The Dancer at World's End

Tricia Durdey

Cinnamon Press
:: small miracles from distinctive voices ::

Published by Cinnamon Press
www.cinnamonpress.com

ISBN 978-1-78864-108-1

British Library Cataloguing in Publication Data. A CIP record for this book can be obtained from the British Library.

Designed and typeset in Adobe Jensen by Cinnamon Press.
Cover design by Adam Craig © Adam Craig.
Cinnamon Press is represented by Inpress

Acknowledgements

With many thanks to Jan Fortune.

To my father, Ronald Wilfred Durdey,
March 1925-January 2016

The Dancer at World's End

Willoughby's new landlady was called Ruby Hoffman.

'I was christened Dora,' she said, standing at the open door of number 7 Gladstone Terrace, her hand outstretched in greeting. 'But I changed my name to Ruby. Dora is such a quiet sort of name—my family got me totally wrong. But they can be excused that, in the circs.'

Ruby Hoffman wore a green beret on which she'd pinned a velvet bird by its feet. 'I'm much more a Ruby than a Dora, don't you think?'

Willoughby had only just met her, so had no opinion about her name or character, nor any idea what the circumstances could be, but he smiled and nodded. She led him into the hall.

'We busk every Friday and sometimes Saturday too, when we feel like it, or when we need the money. I play the accordion and Gregor dances—he's my cousin. Afterwards we go to Antonio's for spaghetti.'

The velvet bird wobbled from side to side as she spoke, mirroring her animation.

His landlady—Ruby Hoffman. She was not as he'd imagined a landlady to be. But then he'd never lived with anyone but his grandmother before. He'd seen the card pinned to the noticeboard of the late-night shop. *Sensible lodger needed to create equilibrium Low rent.* In a reckless moment, tired of living alone another year, he'd rung the number.

Willoughby sat in the window of the café the day after moving into number 7. A sudden snowstorm whirled down in flurries, and as he looked out into the street, they appeared round the corner like two strange birds, carefully treading the icy pavement. There they are, he thought, Ruby and Gregor—was Gregor a Hoffman too? He felt a thrill of excitement.

Gregor carried the accordion box over his left shoulder, leaning away to balance the weight. Ruby held his right arm.

They stopped outside the café where the pavement was wide. Gregor put the box down, opened it and took out the accordion. He helped Ruby ease the straps over the bulk of her coat. She shook out her raggedy auburn hair, looked up at him and, despite the falling snow, she began to play. She smiled as she played and swayed to the rhythm of a waltz, as if the accordion were her partner. Gregor put up an umbrella and held it over her. Willoughby gazed at them through the space in the glass where he'd rubbed away the condensation. He liked the way she played. The music had a haunting, far-away quality. He imagined blue sky, white birds flying in arcs against the sun, flags fluttering over a Punch and Judy show and the waves falling. He spooned up his soup and it dribbled down his shirt as he watched.

A little girl stopped to listen, but her mother pulled her away. People put up umbrellas, or scurried for shelter, a boy ran by with his briefcase held over his head, and someone shouted with excitement. Only one other person watched them as intently as Willoughby—a young woman sheltering by the salvation army hut, her coat drawn close round her, scarf swaddling her neck.

After three songs Ruby stopped playing. Still holding the accordion, she took a bar of chocolate from her pocket and broke off pieces to share with Gregor, as they stood close under the umbrella.

It stopped snowing as abruptly as it had started. The black branches of the sycamore on the street corner dripped melted ice, and the sun slanted bronze light over the blocks of flats behind them. Gregor shook and closed the umbrella and Ruby took a blue cloche hat from her pocket, pulled it on and began to play again. There was the red velvet bird, pinned loosely, bobbing about as she played, as it had done the first time Willoughby met her. Did she always wear a bird on her hat?

With the first bars of music Gregor began to dance—a curious dance—whirling round, almost falling, catching and holding a precarious balance, wild and then controlled.

Someone shouted bravo and applauded, but he continued to dance, lost to everything but the music, spinning and leaping in wild, breathless abandonment. Ruby stopped playing. They looked at each other and laughed. The sun had gone; the winter afternoon was closing in.

Willoughby left the café and stood to one side as they packed up. Around them everyone hurried for buses or the tube. He didn't like to leave. They hadn't picked up their tin of takings, but it looked almost empty. He delved in his pockets and found he only had a few coppers left. It seemed so little, too little to give. Instead he found a paper bag half full of pear drops. As he approached he wanted to say he was sorry he had nothing.

'Willoughby Stone,' Ruby said, looking up from the accordion with the bold, almost challenging, attitude he'd noticed on their first meeting. 'So you found us.'

She took the paper bag he offered, opened it, sniffed the sweets and smiled. She handed him one, but he shook his head.

'I would give you money if I had any,' he said.

'Ah, and it's our birthday today too! So disappointing. We were born on the same day, Gregor and me, nine years and one country apart.'

Blushing with awkwardness, he mumbled happy birthday, and hurried away, too shy to ask if they were going home and should he wait. There wouldn't be enough tonight for spaghetti in Antonio's, and he felt sorry about that. If he'd money himself he could have taken them.

It grew dark with a flurry of hail. Lights went on in the tower blocks at World's End. At the corner of the street he turned to see them moving, laden and slow, in the direction of the river. The hail stung his face. Maybe he could buy them a bottle of wine another day.

Gregor Loeben walked abstractedly, gazing sometimes up at the heavy sky, the criss-crossed tracery of trees, sometimes down at the pavement with its grubby patches of snow. For a moment he stopped altogether, and muttered to himself as if he'd forgotten something, before moving slowly on. Willoughby, who walked some distance behind, stopped too. It was awkward to go so slowly, but he held back, too shy to catch up with Gregor, wishing he had his bicycle so he could speed by unnoticed. He still hadn't been introduced to his landlord. Ruby had been disarming enough.

Gregor wore a long grey coat, his light hair fell over the collar and he carried a cloth bag over his shoulder. He moved quietly, softly, like a cat, Willoughby thought, without the energy of his wild dance that snowy afternoon, but with the same lithe grace. Willoughby followed him down the narrow passageway between the houses, past a patch of early weather-beaten daffodils, and held back, just enough to keep a distance between them.

Two men, their heads close-shaved and scarred, turned into the passageway and strode towards Gregor Loeben as if they knew him. They didn't smile. Gregor stepped back, but they hopped from side to side, mocking him, pretending to let him pass, then blocking the way again. Swiftly the taller man grabbed Gregor either side of his head and spat twice in his face. Gregor lowered his gaze, froze. The other tore the bag from his shoulders and threw it down. Paperback books scattered over the path. The men turned and disappeared between the houses.

Willoughby felt the assault like a blow to his stomach. Flushing with shame for having done nothing to help Gregor, he hurried forward and retrieved his bag. The books were muddied, and he tried to dry them with the end of his scarf and cram them back in.

'I'm sorry,' he said.

Gregor's eyes were glazed with hurt. 'Thank you,' he whispered. He took a handkerchief from his pocket and wiped the spittle from his cheek. His face cleared and he smiled.

'You're our new resident. I saw you from the window last night when you were cycling home.' He reached out his hand to take Willoughby's. His eyes were a startling blue, and there was sweetness in his smile. 'I'm sorry about that little incident. As you see, they're no friends of mine.'

'Do you know them?'

'Let's say I've encountered them once or twice. It's unpleasant, but I have no quarrel with them.'

He spoke carefully, politely, Willoughby thought, as if he came from another age, or was it another country?

'I'll walk home with you,' he said. 'If that's where you're heading.'

'Thank you, my friend, I should be glad of your company.'

They walked in silence. The late afternoon sun lit up the rooftops and chimneys with brilliance, so everything seemed clearer to Willoughby, as if washed and new. Gregor shivered, cleared his throat.

'I have to tell you something.' He stopped walking and turned to face Willoughby, touching his arm. 'I have to tell you I'm not English at all. I'm German. Gregor von Loeben. I dropped the von when I came to England.' He lowered his eyes. 'Often here I'm hated for being German, they spit at me, and I understand, I understand very well, because it was all hideous and hatred is quite deserved. So I prefer to tell people straight away that I'm German. I put my cards face up on the table, as you say in English. Then there can be no misunderstanding.' He swallowed, rubbed a hand across his eyes. 'My father was in the Nazi party, you see—a rather important person. And I met Hitler when I was a child, and all that. I had no idea…' He blinked, shook his head. 'Had I stayed in Germany I could have forgotten it all—the only way to move on, you see. Our German parents are afflicted with great forgetfulness over these matters. But here, in London, I can't forget, and that's why I have to tell you.' His smile was strained. He held out his hand. 'I'm sorry, so sorry.'

'It's not your fault.' Willoughby took his hand. 'You were a kid. You can hardly be held responsible.'

'Ah, but it's not so simple. It's a balance, a careful balance. It's always possible to fall on the wrong side, and once fallen it's very hard to find a way up.' Gregor looked away into the distance. 'But thank you for your understanding.' He reached into his pocket. 'I found this at the market, a good big Jaffa orange. Please have it.' He thrust it into Willoughby's hand. 'Are you lonely, my friend? We're all lonely from time to time. Life can be difficult.' He smiled. 'We have meals at the house. Please join us tonight. All the others do.'

They reached the house. Gregor stopped at the foot of the steps leading to the front door.

'I'm not coming in yet after all,' he said. 'Should you see Ruby, tell her I've gone for a walk. Please tell her I'll be home soon.'

Gregor turned away from the house, walked with great urgency to the end of the street and round the corner. Once he was far enough away, he leant, exhausted, against the wall of the tobacconist shop, feeling the waves of sick embarrassment that came with each confession. It will never be over, never be done with, he said to himself.

An old man ambled out of the shop, stopped, filled his pipe from a tin and tamped down the tobacco. He put the tin in his pocket.

'Good evening, my friend,' Gregor said.

The man glanced at Gregor.

'Life is hard. Guilt weighs heavy.' Gregor didn't know why he said this. It was like being momentarily possessed. The old man looked down, baffled, as if Gregor might be talking about the pipe he held in his hand.

Slowly, Gregor set off for the river. He moved with quiet grace, his head held high, with all the appearance of self-assurance he'd never possessed. I mustn't dwell on it any longer, he thought. Just walk until it passes, and then go home when night falls. I'll cook dinner, as I always do, and maybe Willoughby Stone will join us. Maybe he won't give my confession a second thought. The others never minded, and I'm not important, not important at all, at the end of the day I'm a mere grain of sand in the desert. Willoughby Stone. Willoughby Stone. Willoughby is such an aristocratic name, and Stone, well it makes me think of the earth, the sheer weight of things. He's only a young man, seems very shy. His eyes are full of intelligence. He has that way of really looking at you, taking things in. Not many have that. Unusual.

He reached the river and crossed the road. The tide was low, the mud banks silver in the setting sun. Late afternoon traffic roared in a stream along the embankment as he continued down the stone steps, away from the rush, towards the river's edge. Always the smell of watery decay, of the distant sea, soothed him. He sensed that rhythm in his body, a gentle ebb and flow, that sometimes came into his dreams. Maybe one day I'll come to terms with it all— the shame, the guilt—he thought. But for now it didn't seem possible. It must only be endured.

He noticed a woman standing on the bridge, not far away, a small, motionless figure leaning against the parapet. He sensed she was watching him, and it made him uneasy. As he turned away towards the towers of the power station, a swirling flock of birds filled the sky, each small body seeming to quiver as it wheeled and turned into the fading light, under-wings glowing silver then black again; hundreds of them flying together, like wisps of smoke, like a shimmering cloud, small groups spiralling away and then back, merging, reforming, ever-moving. The noise of the cars and buses faded away. It seemed there was only the strange humming of their wing beat as they came closer, silence when they retreated, and his neck ached with the effort of gazing at them. He couldn't look away. Minutes passed, everything forgotten—only the elation, the joy of flying with them in his imagination.

They left as suddenly as they'd appeared—twilight, the lights shimmering in the water, the shadowy silhouette of the woman on the bridge. He shivered and pulled his coat round him, his feet damp and cold. She seemed to watch him still as he made his way back up the steps. Does she know me? Have we met? He glanced at her, was going to speak, to say good evening my friend, what a wonderful sight, but something stopped him. He turned away to walk along the bank of the river, still reluctant to go home.

Four steps led up to number 7 Gladstone Terrace, where Ruby and Gregor lived with their odd collection of lodgers. The house, with its stone portico over the front door and wrought iron balcony on the first floor, had once been elegant. Now the black paintwork was worn and blistered, the stucco cracked, and brambles burgeoned from the masonry in the basement.

After the first night, unsettled and sleepless, Willoughby decided he would leave in the morning. But it had seemed different when daylight came, so he stayed another night, and then another, and a week later he was still there, in a room on the top floor with his things packed in carrier bags, waiting. He'd give it a little longer. You'll love it here, Ruby had said.

As he unlocked the door, he thought of his strange encounter with Gregor Loeben. It had been weird the way Gregor had stopped in the street and, in a rush, admitted to being German. He'd seemed so distressed too—though wouldn't anyone be after such an assault? Willoughby hadn't known what to say, and was left with a discomfiting sense of having done something wrong.

He stood in the greenish light of the hall, under the dusty chandelier, listening for sounds of the others. That's our tree, our wonderful horse chestnut, Ruby had said the day they met, and now, through the staircase window, he saw a network of dark branches pressing against the glass as if they might shatter it and force a way in. Sometimes, in the winter, the twigs tap in the wind, she'd told him. It's so eerie, especially if you're alone—the east wind all the way from the plains of Siberia. She had spoken in a whisper, as if telling a story to a child.

The house had particular smells and sounds—a damp gaseous stench of drains, a fragrant waft of beeswax polish. In the basement kitchen a tap dripped continuously, the pipes creaked and gurgled. Ruby said the house was like a huge ship that held them all in safety on the wild sea. Willoughby hadn't met the other lodgers yet, and suspected they were as disquieting as Gregor and Ruby. Despite this, he hadn't yet moved on. Something about Ruby made him stay.

'Pear Drop Man!'

He jumped, and she laughed.

She leant over the bannister watching him from the turn in the staircase.

'You didn't hear me. Lost in another world, you are.'

'Gregor will be back later. He told me to tell you,' Willoughby said, in his confusion.

'Oh no. How much later? I suppose he's walking, and now dinner will be late and the Ducks will be waiting with open mouths to be fed.' She ran down the stairs and seized his hand. She was wearing a shapeless mohair jumper over a rose satin evening gown. 'I don't suppose you can cook, can you?'

'Not really.'

'No. I thought not, especially with a couple of mouldy onions, a flabby carrot and some Tabasco sauce. Gregor is a master of the kitchen. He feeds us all on nothing but scraps but it turns into a feast. It's positively Biblical. Has he made his confession about being German? You don't mind too much do you?'

'Why would I?'

'Well people do. Not the Crippled Ducks. To be honest they wouldn't care if he'd been Hitler's best mate. But now he'll walk around the streets as miserable as if the Third Reich was entirely his responsibility. My poor cousin.'

She led him past the mannequin in grey that stood in the turn of the stairs. He, or she—it was never clear—had acquired a new hat, complete with ostrich feathers, since the morning.

'Who are the Crippled Ducks?'

'The people who live here, of course. Oh it's all right, I'm not talking about you. I chose you, and I never choose people I'm sorry for, like Gregor does. He invites the sad, lonely, halt and lame—as well as prostitutes and criminals. It's never boring. You'd better come and meet them. They're at this moment draped round the living room awaiting the return of The Master, as Monica calls him— without irony.'

Letting go of his hand she ran to the top of the stairs and stopped at the door, barring entry with her arm, as if she thought he might burst through.

'Wait. I'll tell you about them first. There are four permanents, but others sometimes come and go. There's SA Pete and The Parson. SA—that stands for South Africa—where he lived for years. He was in prison once for violence, but one night, when he was at rock bottom, he found God by the river. God lifted him from the slough of despond, apparently. He's fine most of the time, except when he breaks, but he prays an awful lot, which is tiresome. The Parson is a dog, a Jack Russell. SA Pete's always trying to make it lie down or give a paw for the saints. Paw dog. Poor dog. All he talks about really is God or dogs. He works in security. Useful.

'Then there's Philadelphia Sullivan. She was a prostitute, I understand, but she's given that up since she moved here. Though she still has endless troubles—always some calamity to moan about. She's so thin I wonder if she offered herself at half price. She's got a girl called

16

Moonlight. Philadelphia will tell you the child was conceived under a full moon, hence the unfortunate name. Moonlight has the deepest voice you've ever heard in a child. Wait until you hear it. She's got a way of watching people, it's unnerving, and she's quite besotted with Gregor. Fortunately she's often staying with Granny.

'Finally, Birdy and Monica—they say they're sisters, but they look nothing like each other. I can't tell you anything about them, not even their real names. But you'll know them because Monica is built like a hockey player and is definitely the chief—bossy cow, and Birdy does nothing but smile and knit. I've never heard her utter a word. She's very tall and sort of unfolds herself when she stands up—you'll see. Gregor found them wandering through a car park in the pouring rain. He brought them back for tea, and they've stayed ever since.

'We're like night and day, Gregor and me.' Her voice lost its careless tone. 'Gregor is kind. Gregor shines so brightly that they all fly towards him like moths. I can be very hurtful, so I'll ask you to forgive me in advance in case I'm ever unkind to you.'

A shadow crossed her face for a moment. Then she laughed and flung open the door.

'This is Willoughby Stone,' she said. 'He lives here now.'

Gregor paused by the houseboats and gazed out across the river to the towers of the power station. Water lapped the quayside. He heard a dog barking and, more distantly, a police siren, but the city seemed to fall away. Gradually, as darkness fell, lights were switched on in the narrow confines of the boats, so he caught a glimpse of a kitchen with blue and yellow cups lined up on a shelf, a brass lamp hanging from the roof, books piled on a table—the life of a stranger. He couldn't imagine how anyone lived in such tiny cramped spaces, yet he had, long ago, lived in a space even smaller, an existence more fragile than anyone who lived in these wooden structures floating on the water. There'd been no food or warmth where he'd once lived, only a heaving mass of flies, shadows on broken walls, and desperate shouts in the night. He had tried to forget, but now the thought of it filled his mind, so he drew in his breath and covered his eyes. The birds flying this evening had seemed like a gift. He had to think of their wild sweeping movement, the way they each knew how to move in synchronicity with the others so they never collided, how they were at once both singular and collective.

A sweet voice broke through the disturbance of memory. A young girl was singing, or was it the radio? Yes, the radio, surely, because he heard a piano and choir, but a young voice too, close by, singing in German. He couldn't make out the words, only the longing and tenderness of her voice, and his own language, loved and hated, spoken only in his dreams. He opened his eyes and saw a girl of about fourteen. She stood at the window of the nearest houseboat, holding a small child in her arms as she looked out across the narrow stretch of water towards him. Mari-Louise. He whispered the name of his sister. Mari-Louise.

Everything had seemed unreal since he'd made his confession to Willoughby Stone. Usually he went home, exhausted, defeated by his struggle for equilibrium, but now everything seemed full of wonder, as if for a moment he'd entered a new world—the miracle of the birds' flight, the sweet song of the young woman with her baby. And before that, the woman who had stood motionless on the bridge—who was she? She seemed familiar to him. He was filled with a sense of wonder and joy. It was rarely like this—the possibility of redemption—and he was always grateful.

The door of the houseboat opened, and Gregor's thoughts were broken by the young woman calling out into the dusk.

'Joey, you coming in now? Joey.'

No, she wasn't German.

18

Distantly, a voice called back, and Gregor, as he climbed the steps to the street, saw the figure of a boy scurrying across the mud.

He would buy treats on the way home; those honey pastries that Ruby adored, chocolate cherries for Philadelphia and coffee creams for the sisters. He'd find something that Willoughby Stone might like, and SA Pete and The Parson too. He had very little money left for the rest of February, but tonight it didn't matter.

Three hours after he'd left Willoughby on the doorstep of number 7, Gregor crossed the road and looked up at the balcony window. A slip of moon hung above the roof between the chimneystacks. The silk curtain was open and he saw SA Pete, his hand raised as if he held something, and then the little dog tottering towards him on its hind legs. A fine rain fell but Gregor didn't move. He could smell the earth for the first time since winter. From the cold damp street it seemed a beautiful room, warm and inviting. Ruby appeared in one of her ridiculous evening dresses with a blanket over her shoulders, and he felt a pang of love for her—Ruby whose troubles were so different from his own. She often dressed for dinner, as if the event should be special, and he had let her down tonight.

She must have sensed he was near. She opened the French window and stepped out onto the balcony, dragging the blanket with her and wrapping it round her shoulders. Her feet were bare and she did a little dance in the cold as if to warm them, then leant against the iron balustrade, peered into the street and called out.

'Gregor. What are you doing out there like a ghost? We've waited ages for you. Come in now. We all so much want you to come in.'

'I'm coming,' he said. He ran across the road and up the steps to the door.

Willoughby lay on his back in bed, sleepless with the cold. He thought about the evening, how Ruby had ushered him into the living room with a flourish and they'd all turned to look at him. He'd entered a large, cold, high-ceilinged room, with the same decaying grandeur as the rest of the house. A French window opened to the balcony, and the ceiling was decorated with an ornate gilded architrave and centre rose. But the plasterwork was chipped and faded, the floorboards painted inexpertly with dark red gloss paint and a border of ivy leaves in green and gold, and scattered with velvet cushions moulting feathers. There was a *chaise longue* covered in fake mink, and a full-length, gilt-edged theatre mirror spotted with mildew.

Ruby took the mink from the chaise and threw it at him.

'Well here you are, Pear Drop Man, welcome to number 7. You might need this. I'm conserving gas.'

They sprawled on cushions amongst an assortment of blankets and looked at him with interest. A small scruffy dog got up, stretched and sniffed his feet. He knew them immediately. Ruby's descriptions had been unkindly perfect.

'Hello,' he said, and patted the dog.

Monica went back to turning the pages of a magazine, Birdy smiled and nodded nervously, Philadelphia stubbed out her cigarette and pretended to scrutinise her nails, whilst appraising him. Only SA Pete stood to greet Willoughby, then called his dog and made her lie down to be combed. Ruby opened a bottle of Spanish red, poured Willoughby a glass, and told him to sit down and relax. He sat, ill at ease, and riffled through a stack of records for something to do.

'Put one on,' Ruby said. 'What music do you like?' But she didn't wait for his answer. She picked a record herself. 'Listen to this voice.' She slipped it onto the turntable and lowered the needle. A woman sang something from an opera. 'Maria Callas—wonderful.'

From time to time Philadelphia spoke and Ruby answered. But she was distracted and kept wandering to the window, pulling back the curtain and looking out, then crouching by the gas fire, which she lit with a match and hunched over to keep warm. He knew she was waiting for Gregor to come home, and couldn't rest. He saw then she was younger than she'd first seemed—maybe only thirty, not much older than him. They waited, desultory and hungry.

Then Gregor had returned and everything changed. He brought the cold air with him, but he stood radiant in the middle of the room, not the same man who'd parted from Willoughby. He put sweets and chocolate on plates in front of people. The room got warmer. Ruby filled their glasses with more wine. Willoughby drank and fell asleep.

When he woke they'd all gone. He was lying on the *chaise* with the fake fur over him. He couldn't recall being sleepy, only the warmth, and the music, which had seemed extraordinarily lovely. It was as if he'd fallen under some enchantment. A candle in a glass jar flickered low. He stumbled upstairs to his room, took off his boots and hung his coat over the chair.

He lay in the cold and thought about them all, the ones she called Gregor's Crippled Ducks, or The Grotesques. They were ordinary people, maybe poor, maybe lonely, people nobody would notice in a street, not even Philadelphia with her thin hungry look and knot of hair. Only Ruby and Gregor would stand out.

After a while he gave up trying to sleep. He got up and put the radio on—the World Service, so low he couldn't make out the words, but the sounds were restful. He emptied his pencils onto the floor, reached into one of his carrier bags for a sheet of paper, and switched on the light. He drew Ruby, her face framed with curly untidy hair, her hat with the fabric bird. He stood back and saw how good a likeness it was. He drew her again and again, from different angles, covering sheets of paper and dropping them to the floor. He took a stick of charcoal and tried to draw Gregor's face, but though he could see the features, the high narrow forehead, intense deep-set blue eyes, it was like trying to form something from air, and the more he tried the more Gregor seemed to slip from his grasp.

He sank back onto his bed exhausted, peeled the orange Gregor had given him and divided it up. As he sucked the juice out of each segment he thought about Gregor, the haunted look in his eyes as he'd made his confession, the hand that reached for his arm, as if begging for deliverance. The episode had left a mark, as if in some inexplicable way he too was involved.

When Moonlight found herself alone in number 7, she took the opportunity to explore the adult world by looking in everyone's room. Sometimes she could tell what people were like by the things they had around them, as if their personality was stamped over everything. Other rooms seemed to belong to nobody particular, and yielded no secrets. She investigated the rooms in strict rotational order. Her mother's was familiar and chaotic, and Monica and Birdy's, with their china animals on every shelf, was of only passing interest—which was good because Birdy was usually at home, sitting on a chair by her bed, surrounded by balls of knitting wool.

Moonlight liked Ruby's room best—it smelt of her perfume. There were dresses, so many, shabby and torn in places, but still gorgeous, with lace trims, satin flounces and embroidered collars. Long chiffon scarves, shot with threads of gold, festooned the wardrobe door, and various hats hung on pegs by the window. She had peacock feathers in a vase and a jewelled box crammed with makeup. A high brass bed was veiled with lace curtains, and underneath were boxes of shoes, slippers and boots.

Gregor's room was as different from Ruby's as it was possible to be. His mattress, on the floor, was covered in a sheet and two grey army blankets. There was an upturned wooden box with a candle in a brass holder on top, and a leather trunk where he stored his clothes, folded neatly and divided into sections. The remarkable thing was the way he'd stacked the paperback books, nine to each stack, vertically and horizontally along the length of one wall, and five stacks high. Moonlight had estimated, it being a long narrow room, that he had over eight hundred books. It was a mystery what they were for, as she'd never seen him reading.

She'd made the most thrilling discovery in SA Pete's room. It wasn't a pretty room, being full of an odd collection of mismatched furniture, but he kept things ship-shape—as her grandmother would say—and there was a cross on the wall over his bed and another on the mantelpiece. In the corner was a ladies' dressing table with a kidney-shaped glass top, a mirror and drawers hidden behind a gathered floral curtain. When she opened the drawers she found nothing more interesting than men's things—a jumble of socks, pants and handkerchiefs, until she reached the bottom left-hand drawer, and there, lying on a folded newspaper, was a gun. It had made her heart race when she discovered it, and since that day she'd felt a thrill every time she opened the drawer to look. At first she dared not touch it, but one day she found the courage to brush the cold metal with her fingertips. After that first tremor of fear, she touched it every time she went to SA Pete's room, with great caution in case she inadvertently found herself pulling the trigger to see whether it was loaded.

It had been spring when Ruby's mother had found her little nephew, Gregor, in the ruins of post-war Germany and taken him over the border to live in Holland. He was just eleven and could remember little of that time, except that he'd believed he was a man. Now, nearly thirty years later, he sat with Moonlight on a park bench under the lime trees.

The daffodils were over and the beds were full of budding wallflowers. He looked at her as she peered into the bag of tangerines he'd bought, and thought, I was even younger than this when Aunt Hedda rescued me. Moonlight seemed so small and young, as he must have been. It seemed a miracle that he'd survived at all.

Moonlight wore bright green eye shadow. Although she was only ten, her breasts seemed to have developed overnight so he assumed she must have borrowed something padded from her mother. He wanted to tell her she was a child, that she should stay young a little longer yet, but he didn't like to dishearten her. She took the tangerines from the bag and lined them up on the bench. There were eight—one for each person in number 7.

'We can eat ours now, if you like?' He gave her the biggest, took one himself and put the rest back in the bag. She peeled it carefully, sniffing the skin with exaggerated delight.

'Who can make the pips fly the furthest? We have to spit them out.'

'You, I'm sure.'

They spat as far as they could.

'One day there'll be a forest of tangerine trees and nobody will know we planted them, by mouth.'

Moonlight, tall and slender as her mother, had deep-set grey eyes and wore her fine blonde hair pulled tightly back from her face, giving her a ghost-like appearance. Her name was apt. At school she changed it to Susan. It was a safer that way, though it involved complications with the teachers.

She scooped the peel into her hands, dug a little hole in the soil with her toe, and buried it, pressing the soil down with her feet.

'Shall we discuss life now?' she said in her low, un-childlike voice.

'If you like.'

'I'll ask you something first.' She pulled up her socks and huddled into her anorak, against the sharp wind. 'Are you ever going to get married?'

'I haven't thought of it yet.'

'You're not queer are you?'

'No.' He smiled. 'You know too much, Moonlight.'

'Of course I know.' She studied his face for a moment. 'Ruby loves you. You could marry her if she wasn't your cousin.' She paused to pick at a scab on her knee. 'Do you mind me asking?'

'No, I don't mind.'

'It's how I learn, isn't it? You said that before, I learn by asking things. Are you lonely?'

'How could I be? I'm hardly ever alone.'

'With all the Crippled Ducks in the house. That's what Ruby calls us. Why crippled and why ducks?'

'Ruby has her own private jokes.'

'Monica says you're sad because of your early years.'

'Monica?'

'Yes. She said your terrible childhood stained your soul.'

'I never realised she thought about me in that way.'

'Oh she does. Monica adores you. You're her saviour. What were your early years?'

'Well Moonlight,' he looked at her and smiled. 'It's hard to explain really. When I grew up in Germany people weren't kind to each other, and it's hard to forget. That's what makes me sad very often.'

'But people still aren't kind. What's different?'

'Some people aren't, no. But it seemed then as if the whole country turned rotten, and nobody realised until it was too late.'

'Because of Adolf Hitler?'

'Partly. He was the King Pin.'

'The King Pin.' She emphasised the words to give them due gravitas. 'You knew Adolf Hitler, didn't you?'

He nodded.

'I thought so.' She was looking at him steadily, her eyes narrowed, as if trying to read his thoughts. It unsettled him. 'Blood and sick stain too, but you see and smell them. You can't see the stains of the soul, can you? Only feel them? Not like blood and sick.'

She fell silent, circling her thumbs around so they clicked.

'Don't do that.'

'Does it make you feel funny?'

'Yes.'

'Watch how I can spin the whole of my body then.' She jumped up and twirled round until she swayed and staggered. She threw herself down beside him again and arched back to face the sky, singing tunelessly to herself. She turned to look him in the eyes again.

'Can we get married when I'm older?'

'I'm afraid there's a very big age difference between us,' he said, kindly.

'How old are you then?'

'Thirty-nine.'

'Men can have babies much older than ladies.'

'Yes, that's true.'

'So we'd be fine then, wouldn't we?'

'We would. Just about.' He stood up. 'Shall we walk home? It's getting cold.'

She took his hand to balance along the wall and jumped off into his arms. 'Again, again,' she said, until at last he told her he couldn't catch her any more, she'd worn him out, and they called at the café to warm up.

'That lady is watching you,' Moonlight said, stopping and clutching his hand as they reached the corner of their street. 'I keep seeing her. She's always around. The Lady in Green, I call her.'

Gregor looked where she was pointing.

'I thought she might be a ghost because she looks so weird, but last time she was there she asked me what your name is, so then I knew she wasn't a dead person.'

'My name?'

'Yes. She asked if I lived in the house. I told her sometimes, and she said she wanted the name of the man who dances, not the one with the dog.'

'What did you tell her?'

'Dave Morris. It's the first name that came into my head because we knew one once. I was too scared to tell her your real name in case she's a spy. Then I said she should mind her own business. Well, I didn't quite say that. I wanted to.' She grabbed Gregor's hand and spun round.

Gregor caught a glimpse of the woman before she turned away and slipped down the alley at the end of the road.

'You look frightened,' Moonlight said, her voice full of melodrama. 'It's all right. She won't know you're German.' She kissed the back of his hand. 'Unless you tell her.'

Gregor stood alone by the French window and gazed over the dark streets. Moonlight had a way of speaking the truth. She won't know you're German, she'd said, knowing this was what kept him awake at night, even though he'd never told her—had he?

I've hardly been back to Germany, but I know you won't take that as an excuse. Is it my father? Have you come to tell me you've found him? No, you're right, my father never stood trial like the others did. He disappeared, you see. And I was so young. I know it's no excuse. They say the sins of the father are visited upon the son for generations. I was only a child, eight years old. My father disappeared before the war was even over.

He realised, when he stopped muttering to himself, that it was unlikely the woman in green knew anything about his father, especially as Moonlight had given a false name. Dave Morris! He shouldn't let fear infect his thoughts. He moaned aloud, without realising.

He didn't hear Ruby come into the room until she stood behind him on tiptoe, and rested her chin on his shoulder, her arms round his waist. He put his hands over hers.

'You're there,' he said.

'What's wrong?'

'Nothing.'

'Nothing? How can you say that when you stare into the dark for so long and talk to yourself?'

Gregor sat at the kitchen table holding an envelope addressed to Mr David Morris—the handwriting small and precise. He turned it over, sniffed the paper, held it up to the light. He felt sick. His hands shook as he opened it.

She wrote that she'd been searching for singular people. She had seen him busking many times and wanted to meet. She had a space in an old warehouse on Butler's Wharf, where she worked, writing plays and directing theatre. *I trust you will come. I would like to know more about you. You will find me there every day from eight in the morning.* She signed her name *Leda Godwin*.

Ruby came into the kitchen and found him staring into space. She stood behind him and read the letter lying on the table.

'David Morris. Why the hell does she think you're called David Morris?'

'Moonlight told her.'

'Marvellous. Inspired. You don't look like a David at all. You're far too *singular*.' She filled the kettle and lit the hob. 'I don't trust her.'

'You never trust anyone,' Gregor answered.

'I do, I trust SA Pete, even though he's a criminal. And I trust Willoughby Stone, and Monica and Birdy, and even Philadelphia up to a point. But this is creepy. How come I never saw her if she's always watching us busking? What's she like? Does she look fun?'

'I saw her once, hardly more than a glimpse. Small, insignificant.'

'Maybe she's a murderer, and at last your punishment for being German will be meted out. What a relief for us all that will be.' Her laughter was strained. 'Do you want tea? Toast? Best eat and drink while you still can.' She took the cups and saucers out of the cupboard. 'Oh no, don't look so distraught. It won't be helpful, you know, meeting her. I'm not serious about your punishment darling.'

'What if it might help to meet her?'

'You're so stubborn.' A cup slipped from her hand and smashed on the floor. 'Now look what you've made me do.'

They'd made enough money that day to go to Antonio's for dinner. Gregor wore a brown suit and navy school tie, with a crest of a lion, he'd found in the Oxfam shop.

'After dinner I'll visit Leda Godwin,' he said.

'No,' Ruby replied. 'By then it will be late.' She flung her kingfisher blue fake fur over her jeans. 'We're going out for fun, not for work. Enough work has been done this week.'

They walked into a windstorm that shook the trees so the branches rattled. Ruby continued to argue, her voice snatched away in the wind. He turned to her, held her close until she grew still.

'Don't worry.'

'I'm not a child,' she pushed him away. 'I know you. Every pain of yours strikes me here.' She pointed to her stomach. 'How can I not worry? I'm sick with it.'

Antonio's, a small, windowless place, smelt of garlic, olive oil and, faintly, of sewage from the drains. The restaurant was almost full—a group of girls celebrating a sixteenth birthday, a family with three small children, and a couple holding hands across the table. Gregor and Ruby sat in front of a mural of mountains, olive trees and deep blue sea. Plastic grapes drooped over them.

Ruby sipped red wine and watched the other diners, listening to conversations. Closing the menu, she called Antonio, and then raised her glass and smiled at Gregor.

'So glad we're away from the Ducks for an evening.'

Antonio came over and gave a little bow. Ruby pushed her mass of curls away from her face and smiled at him.

'Smells delicious, so good,' she said. 'As always. And we'll have the same as usual, with more salad and extra cheese. Oh yes and bread and olives to start.'

She played with the hot wax from the candles, nudging it round, letting it harden on her fingers, scattering it over the table, and quietly hummed a fragment of melody.

'Gregor, I've had an idea for a new song for us. Listen.'

But he wasn't listening. He was looking at the entrance.

'She's just come in,' he said. 'I'm sure it's her.'

Ruby turned round.

'Leda Godwin. But I'd never have guessed from what you said. She's not insignificant. Don't you ever notice women? Yes, after all I have seen her watching us. And she never leaves anything. Not even ten pence.'

They watched Leda Godwin take off a long green coat and sit at the only free table. She took a notebook and pen from her bag and bent her head over the pages. For a while she wrote, then looked up, gazed at the wall, blinked, and then back to her writing.

Gregor wanted to be invisible. Seeing her, he realised he'd been wrong, wanting to meet. It had felt different in his imagination. Faced with the possibility, he knew Ruby was right. It would do no good. And there was the disquieting sense that she was familiar. That he might have met her before.

'She's seen you but she's pretending not,' Ruby said. 'I think I'll invite her to come over.'

'No.'

'I will.' Her face was defiant as a child's. 'Just like you to change your mind at the final moment. I'd like to know about her before she finds out about you. Otherwise I'll feel haunted.'

Leda Godwin looked in their direction. Ruby waved to attract her attention.

'Don't. You're being reckless. You said you wanted an evening of peace.'

'I did, but I'm about to sabotage it, before anyone else does.'

She sprang up and went to Leda's table. He saw them exchange words. Leda stood up. She's tall, not small, he realised, seeing her next to Ruby. Almost as tall and gaunt as Birdy.

'I have to tell you my name isn't David Morris,' he said, standing to greet her.

'Leave it, Gregor,' Ruby said. 'It's not important.'

'I have to confess I'm not even English, so couldn't have an English name,' he rushed on. 'My name is Gregor von Loeben, but I dropped the von long ago.'

Leda looked him in the eyes. It was too much and he looked away, down at her feet in the green leather lace up shoes.

'Gregor von Loeben,' she repeated. 'So you're German.'

'Yes.'

He felt the familiar pressure and roaring in his head, felt he might fall.

'Yes, I see that now,' she said. 'I hear it in your voice too.'

Everything went dark. He felt Ruby grab his arm.

'Jealousy is useless, don't you think?' Ruby said to Willoughby as she sat on the steps that led down to the river, hugging her knees and gazing across the water to the silent big dipper in the funfair. 'I mustn't think about it any more.'

She had persuaded Willoughby to go for a picnic with her, despite it being early March, and the sunlight intermittent.

'There it is. There was a terrible accident there, in the pleasure gardens, and they closed it.' She pointed to the distant dipper. 'That was the year we moved to number 7, Gregor and me. It was such fun, until that happened. We used to go at night. Brilliant. But I mustn't think about that either.' She trailed a little insect with her finger. A burst of laughter and applause came from a riverboat. 'They're having a nice time.' She took a small pocketknife and an avocado from the bag she carried over the shoulder. 'Do you want some of this?'

'I've never had one. I've looked at them in the shops and wondered what you do with them.'

'Cut it in half and spoon it up with a teaspoon. It's supposed to have olive oil and salt. But I don't carry olive oil, salt, or teaspoons actually.'

She sliced the avocado into four segments, pulled away the stone, and gave him half. 'Chew it away from the skin, or peel it with your fingernails. It's good for you, so they say.'

The flesh seemed soapy and tasteless. Willoughby ate one segment and left the rest on his lap, wondering how to dispose of it.

'Jealousy doesn't do anything but make everything worse.'

'But sometimes it's just how you feel, and there's no point in pretending it isn't.' He looked down at the avocado. There were black bits on it, like a bruise.

'You're right. Jealousy and guilt—useless and irksome. One night SA Pete asked me to pray. I decided to go along with it even though I was worried I'd upset him by giggling. We knelt down together on the wooden floor, like a couple of old choristers. I said, if you exist, God, if you're there at all, please send us somebody who will help Gregor. And stop me being jealous of them when they appear. Because I can't help him myself, even though I've tried for years—tried until I feel stark crazy wild.' She shook her hair from her face and pushed it under her beret. 'Friday was the night of the dinner with this woman, Leda Godwin—the night of the storm. I told you, she wants to know Gregor's story. I've got to tell you the rest because it got more and more surreal. Are you listening?'

'Of course I'm listening.'

'Good. Well I invited her to come to our table, because I always think if something's going to happen we might as well get on with it rather than wait in trepidation. I thought Gregor was going to be sick, but he recovered.

'To begin with she was serious, and treated it like an interview. She's a writer for the theatre, or so she said, and she might want to work with us, with Gregor anyway. She said I was too pretty and noisy. Imagine. Me! She was talking about the wonders of theatre, how it can redeem, transform…all those things I'm sure I should know, my mother being a choreographer—but I've never told you that have I?'

'Not yet, I hardly know you, remember,' Willoughby said.

'Well that's not important now, I'll tell you about my amazing Mama another day. Leda Godwin cut her pizza into small segments and ate each piece with her fingers, and after she'd eaten a quarter of the pizza, she wiped her hands very thoroughly on the napkin, sat back and looked from Gregor to me. She said to me, you're not German, are you? I can see that. I told her she was wrong because I'm German on my mother's side. My father was Dutch and Spanish, and I was born in Holland. Then she had the cheek to tell me my English is impeccable, which of course I know, excellent linguist that I am. I told her it might be dangerous to go digging everything up, turning it round and investigating it without considering our feelings—that she was no doctor and had no right to interrogate Gregor. And very quickly she said, but I do consider, most certainly I do, and I give far more attention to people than any doctor. And Gregor just sat looking so sad and uncomfortable it might have made me mad if I hadn't done my best to ignore him.

'And what will you give in return? I asked and I looked her in the eye. She looked back at me, so intensely it felt uncomfortable, so I lit a cigarette for something to do. To search for the truth, she said, out of the blue. The truth.

Heaven forfend! That's when she told me I was too noisy and too pretty to work with. So I said I could put a bag over my head if it would help.

'After that it got even funnier. A group of girls on the next table burst out singing happy birthday and Antonio brought a cake with sparklers sputtering and everyone applauded, so that distracted us for a while. Then Leda tidied the remains on her plate and looked at me and said, the bag won't be necessary. Can you imagine? No sense of humour at all. Not necessary because she's not interested in my story. But she should be interested. She's missing the best by excluding me. My life story and Gregor's are so entangled; she'll never know the full picture of his without mine.

'We were just getting ready to leave when a boy came in with a bunch of white roses. He was selling them to the ladies and he was going round each table. He looked like a cat, a wide face with cheekbones, almond-shaped green eyes and very slicked back blonde hair. When he saw Gregor with Leda Godwin and me, one on either side of him, he smiled. He started to sing that song from the film *Cabaret*, the one that Joel Grey does with the two ladies. You must know it?'

'No. I never saw *Cabaret*.' Willoughby said.

'Oh you should see it. Joel Grey is the compère and he holds hands with two German girls, who are really men dressed in dirndl skirts, with golden plaits and grotesque faces. It goes like this, and I swear this is what the man with the roses did, except the bundle of roses bobbed about as he sang.' She sprang to her feet and sang... 'And the girls skip around him in this hideous way, and so it goes on.' She sat down again.

'Anyway, Gregor looked horror-stricken, and Leda Godwin said, very coldly, please go away. I burst out laughing, and the more serious the two of them became the worse it got. The man with the flowers just stood there and kept saying, oh I'm so sorry, I don't know what got into me, but I love *Cabaret* and then seeing you three... That just made it worse. So I bought a rose each for Gregor and Leda Godwin, and told him he'd better go before our personal Cold War started. Gregor kept saying, how did he know I was German, as if the man was a clairvoyant? Leda Godwin tried to reassure him. All that was going on when water started to drip onto our table from the ceiling, right on the middle of Leda Godwin's head. She didn't notice at first, but I did, I was entranced, waiting to see what would happen. She leapt up, as if she'd been electrocuted. A big Italian drama followed, with people rushing around with pans to catch the water, moving tables, shouting upstairs to find out what was wrong. A tap had been left on in a bathroom, a plug in the washbasin, and everything had flowed over. And so we left—out into a storm, me clutching two roses. Leda Godwin got into a taxi and sped away, leaving us battling an umbrella in the wind.'

Willoughby smiled. 'What then?'

'I wanted to go out, oh so much, and tell someone about it, and laugh and get drunk. But that wasn't possible. My darling cousin was much disturbed, so we went back and made cocoa for the Crippled Ducks, and I wished you were in. Where were you? Philadelphia arrived back in a taxi, drunk. At least she wasn't as miserable as she usually is, but she doesn't exactly lift the heart. And so it is, you see. Number 7 is a kind of house for the deranged. Help me God.'

She shivered and fell silent, tucking her hands under her arms.

'Life is hard enough for Gregor without the guilt,' she said at last. 'If only he could forget. Our parents were so different and I'm a constant reminder. The sins of the father are visited upon the son. He says that too often, when really there should be no cause to say it at all.'

Willoughby tentatively put his arm round her.

'Ah, a shoulder to lay my weary head on.'

'What about your parents?' he asked. 'When we first met, you said something about them being excused in the circumstances.'

'Did I? I'll tell you another time. I'm tired with it all now. You should see *Cabaret* though. It's one of the best—"*divinely decadent, darling.*"' She gave a theatrical gesture with her hand. 'You have to imagine I'm holding a long cigarette holder. I'll take you if it's ever screened round here again.'

Gregor slowed to a standstill in the middle of the street. *I understand now. Why didn't I realise before?* The market stalls were closing soon and he should buy his provisions. He should look for the little gifts he sometimes put in their rooms—it always made Moonlight and Monica especially happy. But he hadn't been able to think clearly since the night at Antonio's, and over and over again he revisited the scene in the restaurant with Leda Godwin—the boy with his bundles of white roses, a sparkle in his almond eyes as he sang. He'd thought he was being funny. It should have been funny, but only Ruby had giggled, then laughed hysterically. It must be written over my face, I'm the son of a Nazi, Gregor had said, when they got home. But Ruby said that was nonsense. The boy with the roses was too young to give a damn about Hitler and Germany. He just liked *Cabaret*, as she did too. *I shouldn't let fear take hold. The boy must have known me, of course. I've met him somewhere, I'm sure of it. Did he once come to the house with Philadelphia? I must have told him then that I was German.*

The market was almost over; a grocer packed the remaining food into boxes, and hefted them into trucks, leaving the gutters to the debris of bruised apples and cabbage leaves, the smell of bins and rotting fruit. Gregor found good things cheaply, or free, just before the market closed—the remains of fish sold before it went off, bananas just going brown, a cabbage that had rolled into the gutter, two potatoes, an orange—enough to feed anyone who turned up at number 7. Now he'd resolved in his mind the situation with the boy, he wandered down the street, picking up the waste fruit and vegetables and dropping them into his bag with quiet concentration, and murmuring to himself. It would be nice to find chocolate biscuits going cheap for Birdy, or a colouring book for Moonlight. Spring was in the air, the evening lighter. For a moment his troubled mind cleared, and happiness burst in like a ray of sun.

He crossed the road between the empty stalls. A man and a girl sauntered towards him, but though Gregor gazed in their direction, he was pre-occupied, wondering what he might find as a gift for Ruby, and didn't notice them until they were nearly upon him. Startled, he saw the girl had the same honey coloured hair as his nurse, Johanne, all those years ago. He smiled.

'Do you want a photo?'

'Sorry,' Gregor answered, confused. 'A photo?'

The man sneered. Gregor smelt the greasy sweat of him; saw his eyes narrowed, the yellow teeth. He stepped backwards as the face came closer.

'Watch who you stare at, Fuck Head.'

As they walked away, Gregor saw the girl glance back at him—her expression of prurience and revulsion. What had he done?

He dropped to his knees. When his head cleared and light returned, he saw them disappearing down the passageway between the shops, and then he remembered the boys. Every day at school in Holland they had called him a German Pig. Sometimes they'd dragged him to the toilets, pushed his face into the shit until he felt he was drowning, then flushed water over him and laughed as he rose gasping. He had cried at night in his little room in the house his aunt had taken him to, the house in Amstelveen where he was meant to be safe. He told nobody but Ruby about the boys. She was so little then, hardly old enough to understand, but she'd crept into his bed and put her small arms round his neck. Pigs are sweet, she'd whispered in his ear, I love pigs. I love you with all my heart, Gregor.

His face burnt with shame and his hands trembled. He should be careful not to stare at people and smile. It disconcerted them. My name is Gregor von Loeben, he whispered. But I dropped the von. It's easier that way.

He walked in a daze towards the ruined church—it had been bombed in the Blitz but now there was a garden all round, and it always felt to him a holy place. As he drew nearer he quickened his pace, desperate to reach the safety of its confines. Once there, he sank back against the wall of the nave and gazed up at the dark tracery of the east window and the sky beyond it, watched the sky deepening into twilight blue. He fell into a trance.

Six o clock, six-thirty—evening, the air damp with the softness of spring, a winter jasmine flowering against the wall, somewhere in the trees a blackbird singing. Light rain fell and the pavements gleamed, throwing up the scent of wet stone and the earth.

Leda Godwin had given him all her attention that night. Nobody before had wanted to know his story. They'd look away discomfited, or, like Ruby, would try to protect him. But there was no safe place. In truth, Ruby knew that and it frightened her.

Never had such intense interest been focused on him before the night at Antonio's. It was extraordinary, and he realised how he'd longed for this. Yes, there is a story I can tell her, he thought, and something Leda Godwin can give in return by listening. At what cost, Ruby would argue? Why dig it all up again? But that didn't matter, for nothing had ever been laid to rest. There was no question of sparing himself. He was already too deeply lost.

It was almost morning when Gregor let himself into number 7. He'd forgotten he was meant to cook for everyone. They would wait for him, anticipating the dishes he'd lay out on the table. Ruby would have no patience and certainly wouldn't cook. She might butter some toast for consolation, and in the end they would shamble back, disappointed and hungry, to their rooms. Anxiety for him would gnaw at Ruby. She'd open a bottle of wine, drink, take out the accordion, improvise on it a while, then put it aside. She'd put on a record and sing, drink until the bottle was empty. In the end she'd fall asleep. She always slept easily.

Silently he climbed the stairs, opened the door of Ruby's room and crept in, listening for the sound of her breathing. Ah, there it was, soft and regular. He was sometimes afraid he'd find her dead. It was absurd, even neurotic of him—he knew that. Why should a perfectly healthy young woman die in her sleep? But those nights he couldn't rest unless he was certain she was alive. He glanced behind the curtain around her bed and saw her, lying on her back, one arm thrown over her face, the way she'd slept as a child. He was glad—she hadn't worried too much then about his absence. He closed the door, and went to his room.

'Gregor thinks better in a room that looks like a prison cell, no furniture at all,' Ruby told people. 'And all those books. He never reads them. Just buys more and more. He hopes he'll absorb the words into his mind, like some kind of osmosis.'

Gregor made his way past the wall of books and stepped over his mattress to stand by the window. After walking for so many hours he felt bitterly cold, his legs throbbed and he had the familiar sense that he was floating in the stillness. Looking across the street to the houses opposite, the angled lines of rooftops and chimneys beyond, the city seemed vast, stretching into the far distance—countless rooms, countless lives. He was floating in a great universe, and perhaps, after all, that universe would look kindly on him.

He heard footsteps on the stairs, the front door closing, and Willoughby Stone walking briskly away from the house. He always left early for the school, where he was caretaker and cleaner, sometimes on the bicycle he chained to the railings overnight. With a stab of guilt Gregor remembered the promised meal last night. He'd make reparation tonight; prepare a feast more elaborate and delicious than he'd done for a while. It would be all right.

He took off his shoes and lay on his back, the blanket pulled round him. Sometimes he imagined walking into cold river water, letting the current carry him downstream. Those sleepless nights it helped him to let go. When Ruby played the accordion, when the crowds watched him dance, he would be there, floating, and everything for a moment would fragment, no longer embodied—the relief of oblivion. On the edge of sleep, he half-remembered something, and it gnawed at him. Where was it? Why was he seeing that desolate place amidst a desert of ruined buildings? It must be a memory from the last months before he was rescued from Germany. In his mind he saw the remaining brick wall of a factory. High up, a ventilation fan spun slowly in the wind, and the cord that had once controlled it dangled, redundant. Sometimes the blades of the fan turned one way, sometimes the other. His family had gone and he was entirely alone and lost. Gregor tried to remember more clearly, but it was like looking into white mist, struggling to make sense of the shapes that loomed towards him. A miasma of despair hovered at the edge of his consciousness, like the remnants of a bad dream.

He dropped into sleep for but a moment. There was no colour or sound in the vision that rose out of the darkness— the profile of a Nazi, walking like a dead man through the boundless waste of the ruined city: all hope gone forever.

He shot up, stricken with horror.

I remember now, I see it, he whispered to himself—*that wall with the extractor fan high up in the gable, the blades that turned this way, then that way. I lived in a cellar and the days were hot, so it must have been summer. I had to wriggle between two beams to get there. But where was it? Why wasn't I at home?*

40

His bedroom door opened and Ruby stood, like a ghost in her white nightgown, dazed with sleep, an eiderdown draped round her shoulders.

'You shouted out,' she said. 'Are you all right?' She came in, shut the door, and knelt down beside him. 'Oh no, you're shivering cold.' She pulled the blanket round him, and sat close, wrapping her eiderdown over them both. 'It's all right, it's all right.' She rubbed his hands to warm them. 'I'm so glad you're safe home.'

He stared into the darkness. He remembered how flies had crawled everywhere, millions of them, so that, from a distance, they looked like a covering of soft black velvet that vibrated with their commotion. He shivered with revulsion. His bed was made of sacking, and he slept beside an old lady who cried and groaned. The papery skin of her face smelt of soil. Above their hiding place was a rose-papered parlour that opened to the sky, with a wooden crucifix hanging over the mantel. A flight of stairs led nowhere, a window hung in space. Outside, bony children with big teeth searched the mountains of rubble.

'It was only a dream,' Ruby whispered. 'Rest now, darling. You're here—here in London. It's over.'

Emerging from the hiding place Gregor had held tight to his sack, but a big boy rushed at him and snatched it away. The boy sprang from wall to wall, strong and lithe as a monkey. Chasing after him, Gregor stumbled and fell. When he stood up, his knees dribbled blood. The boy had gone.

He'd crouched on a windowsill and cried. The boy had stolen the pieces of coal he'd found that morning, and his precious sack. When his crying ceased except for the occasional sob, he stayed, still as a statue, staring towards the horizon, where the broken city met the tin-coloured sky.

He wanted to drift away, sleep forever, but Ruby was calling him back, whispering his name.

'I'd never have got lost if the boy hadn't stolen my sack,' he said.

'What boy?' Ruby asked. 'There's no boy. You're still dreaming.'

If the boy hadn't stolen his sack he'd never have crouched so long on the windowsill, nor seen the man who walked down the street into his line of vision. He knew the man was his father by the way he walked, upright, rigid in his long grey coat. 'Wait for me, Father.' Gregor called out, slithering down from his perch.

'Wait for me.'

It was over. He was back in his room in number 7, wrapped in blankets, lying beside Ruby.

'It's all right now,' she said. 'Let's try to sleep again.'

He felt her warmth, seeping into his cold skin. It seemed as if he'd been cold for ages.

'I thought it was Father—the man I followed through the city. I followed him until we reached a bombed-out church. I kept calling. When at last he turned round I saw he was a stranger.'

'It doesn't matter now.' Ruby put her arm over him and snuggled close. 'It was over long ago.'

'Listen. I want to tell you,' he insisted.

She sighed.

'Are you listening?'

'Yes. As long we can sleep when you've told me.'

'I thought he was Father and when I saw his face, it was like being struck. I kept on pulling at his sleeve because I couldn't believe it wasn't him. The stranger told me to go away, and jabbed me with his stick. I haven't anything for you, he said. I still tried to follow. He said, if you carry on following me I'll break your neck.

'I realised I was lost. There was nothing to do but walk and hope I'd find my way back to the old woman. As I walked, people streamed towards me with their heads bowed low. I asked where they were going, but their eyes were blank, and nobody spoke.'

He was quiet. It was over. He sensed Ruby, waiting, slowly letting go. Her body softened, grew heavy against him. Sleep and consolation came.

My name is Gregor von Loeben, he murmured. The sound of his name comforted him, so he said it again. *Gregor von Loeben. My father's name was Ernst von Loeben; my mother's name was Gitta von Loeben. My sister's name is Mari-Louise von Loeben.*

My name is Gregor von Loeben. Von Loeben. Von Loeben.

Willoughby Stone went early to the primary school where he worked as a caretaker. He brought in the sacks of coke, stoked the boiler, emptied the waste paper and swept the floors. At break he brought in the crates of milk and minded the children in the playground. The shy children called him Mr Willoughby. They stayed beside him, wanted him to draw things for them—horses or astronauts. At the end of the day he watched them run through the school gates to their mothers.

After they'd gone home, he sometimes studied their drawings on the walls. They drew pictures of themselves. The infants made squiggles, circles with eyes, stick hands and fingers.

When he looked at the children they didn't look away as adults did. They'd stare and he'd pull faces until they laughed. He loved their open faces. They couldn't hide. If God existed, he would look like the children, their faces translucent, an inner light shining through. Sometimes he saw moments of the same light in adults. He had seen it, briefly, in Gregor Loeben and Ruby Hoffman when they caught each other's eye—and he felt excluded then from their private world. How could he capture that luminosity in his drawings?

Drawings of Ruby covered the floor of his room in number 7—Ruby, her arms round the accordion, her face animated, Ruby in her long, embroidered coat, her hat with the velvet bird, and basket decorated with plastic roses. He'd caught the essence of her every time.

After work Willoughby walked by the river between the two bridges where the houseboats were moored. There were pots of purple and gold crocuses in the windows of the boats, and washing was strung out to dry along the deck. Often a young boy played by himself at the water's edge. The sun shone and the tide was low.

Along the muddy bank he saw Ruby. She wore a patchwork coat with a trim of black lace, and a black beret, and carried a canvas bag over her shoulder. She looked cold and shrunken with misery, but seeing him, her face lit up. He thought it would be nice to go back to the house together. They'd buy chocolate biscuits and make tea, and perhaps they would be alone for a little while. He went down the steps to the strand.

'Hello Willoughby. Here we are, by the river again,' she called.

'I like it. You can smell the sea.'

She sniffed the air. 'I don't know. Maybe. Do you like the sea?'

'Yes.'

He said he would carry her bag as they walked together.

'I was looking for things. Driftwood burns so nicely, but sometimes I find other things too. Coloured glass, smoothed by the water so it's like crystal, once a little china doll, not even broken. That was my best find. I made clothes for her, just like mine. Then I sold her.'

She slithered trying to get her grip on the mud, and he helped her up the steps. Her black ankle boots were streaked with a strand of weed.

'Oh damn it. I'm always so clumsy when I'm unhappy, and I'm so unhappy today,' she said, turning to him with sorrowful eyes. 'I quarrelled with Gregor.' She put her hand to her cheek, theatrically. 'You watch people, don't you Willo? I've seen you, sitting there, calmly taking it all in. What do you see when you look at him?'

'Gregor? I don't know. I don't get him. He seems kind. I've never met anyone so kind. But it doesn't quite add up, if you know what I mean.'

'That's the extraordinary thing. He's always been like that. Kind to his mother, and she was awful, believe me, kind to the Crippled Ducks, even to a dead rat we found one day when we were children and he insisted we bury. We had to have a funeral for it. Yes, we were very young then, but even I thought it was going too far, writhing with maggots as it was. If Adolf Hitler rose from the dead and walked in here, he'd even be kind to him, asking what troubled him, and making him scrambled egg on toast. But guilt weighs on him like a mountain range of boulders. I get scared. It's so hard to keep him safe, and now Leda Godwin threatens to dig everything up that should be left forgotten.'

'And that's why you had a row?'

'Yes. He said he wasn't happy to settle for a lie. Happiness isn't a lie, I told him. Why had he decided to wallow in misery and guilt, I asked? Because I need to unburden myself and I don't know any other way, he said. I hugged him and said he had to be very careful. But he told me he was strong and I needed to let him go. But he's not strong, Willoughby, not strong enough. He never has been.'

They walked in silence, crossed the road.

'Let's go home. You can have tea in my room,' he said, hoping to console her.

'That would be nice. If you're kind to me I can forget it all for a while.'

'It's a good room,' she said, as they settled in. 'I always liked this view, the rooftops, the chimneys and that roof garden with the pots, can you see it there, between those houses and the tree? Have you seen the ginger cat?'

'Yes, impossibly balanced, like a circus performer.'

He boiled the kettle and made tea in the yellow pot his grandmother had given him, opened the packet of biscuits.

'It was a sad kind of day,' she said. 'But now I feel it's much improved.'

Outside a van door slammed and an engine started. Sun lit the rooftops and the edges of the chimneys. A jackdaw on the chimney opposite shook its feathers. Ruby picked up his sketchbook, opened it.

'You've drawn me.' She laughed. 'Lots of times.'

He blushed.

'I draw people all the time—the children at school, and the others in this house and people in cafes. I tried to draw Gregor, but I can't see him.'

'See him?'

'I mean really see. Every drawing I made was wrong, so I tore them up.'

'But you can see me?'

He nodded.

'When I close my eyes, I can't see Gregor's face, I only see the way he moves. Nothing is specific enough, if you know what I mean.'

She turned the pages slowly.

'You're very good. Mama used to draw me. She'd hide her drawings away, and I found them once in a box at the back of her wardrobe. I was so angry. I felt as if she'd been watching me all the time. It was like having a guard. My grandfather understood her though. She has to, Dora, he said. That was before I changed my name to Ruby. It was when I understood for the first time what she'd been through.' She shook her head. 'Do you have to draw too?'

'I guess I do.'

'Why? What is it makes you?'

He thought for a moment.

'A kind of anxiety, I think. When I draw I know people better, and when you know someone you fear them less.' He felt himself blushing again.

'Or maybe you fear them more? It might have been fear with Mama too, for a different reason.'

They heard Moonlight's footsteps running up the stairs and glanced at each other.

'A weird child. Have you drawn her?'

'Not yet.' He hesitated. 'What happened to your parents? You haven't told me.'

'Oh, my mother is still in Holland, an old lady, living her fierce life.' She looked down into the mug that she held on her knee and swilled the tea round. 'I never knew my father.'

She saw his eyes fill. The tears surprised her. There was no need for them. She hadn't told him what really happened. He blinked them away.

'It's all right. I can't miss what I never had, Pear Drop Man.'

'After I've drawn someone I do feel as if I know them better,' he said at last. 'And then sometimes I can't see, like with Gregor.'

'Do you know me better?' She laughed at his discomfort. 'Gregor who walks with the weight of history on his shoulders—you'd have to be a master to draw him.'

She went to him, put her hands on either side of his face.

Gregor walked by night. Light gleamed on the black river and he stood for a moment, feet on the edge of the quay. *Father.* He spoke his thoughts in a low voice, as he often did when he walked alone. *My father. Where are you? Out there, in the darkness.*

If only he could see his father clearly it might be possible to understand. But even if it were possible to go back thirty years, he would only see him through a child's eyes, glazed with admiration and fear. The anatomy of evil, the call to Nazism, would still be impossible to comprehend. Had his father committed evil, or only followed those who did? What was the difference? There remained the conviction that he, Gregor, must atone for him.

Mother insisted you were a good man. She often challenged me to argue so she could silence me. Your father, Ernst von Loeben, was a great man, good and courageous, she'd say. He believed with all his heart in Adolf Hitler, our beloved Führer. Unlike other men, he saw it bravely through to the end. That is what everyone has forgotten.

47

Ernst held fast to his ideals and beliefs when others betrayed their leader and their country. *They're all cowards, every one of them.*

When Gregor had argued gently that his father disappeared when all was lost, she had turned her back on him like a petulant child and refused to speak.

Oh, Father, what's the truth? What did you do—to others, to my sister? If you came back from the dead, would remorse eat at your heart, or would you still make a case for the Third Reich? Speak to me. Speak in my dreams if no other way.

Gregor found he'd walked a long way up the river without noticing. He crossed to the south bank, to the old tea and spice warehouses, redundant now. He turned down a passageway that led away from the wharf to a yard, enclosed on three sides by high brick walls. It was dark, except for the sodium-night-sky and a doorway, dimly lit, in the far corner. He thrust his hands deep into his sleeves for warmth. In his mind he saw himself as a little boy of six, wearing a grey coat with a moleskin collar. *I'm holding my sister's hand and we're looking for Father. We've just got off the streetcar. It's a cold damp day and the chimneys of the foundry are lost in the fog.*

Through great open doors of the foundry he remembered seeing a cavernous space that gleamed with machinery, great steel rollers, a rig of scaffold reaching into darkness. There were shouts and the shriek of a whistle. In the gloom, creatures had scuttled back and forth like rats. They had stark faces and naked heads. *They're only girls.* He heard the pity and horror in his sister's voice. He had seen then—but was that how it was, had he remembered clearly? Words came into his head. *Ostbeiter. Slaven bind sklaven.* His father speaking on the telephone. *Slaven bind sklaven.*

As he crouched in the doorway of a warehouse, the meaning of the words crashed into his mind—*workers from the East, Slavs are slaves.* He shivered.

He'd arrived, by accident it seemed, at the address Leda Godwin had given—a complex of warehouses where the actors and dancers lived and worked. She'd said she had the entire top floor, rent-free as there was no heat and little light. It was too late to disturb her. He would write a note. He delved into his canvas bag for pen and paper and rested the pad on his knee. Damp chill seeped from the wall into his clothing.

Dear Miss Godwin,

Since our meeting I can't rest. Tonight I walked without knowing where I was going, without a plan or a map, and found my way here, as if it was meant to be, sitting in the yard of your warehouse with my back against the brick wall. I would like to tell you my story. I need to tell you. Since I met you, dreams come to me in the night and haunt my days. Whatever I'm doing, I forget. I can't concentrate. Words come in German and I find I'm talking to myself.

After the war I was rescued by my Aunt Hedda and taken to Holland, and a new life began. I knew I was German—the Dutch children at school had special and awful ways of dealing with me. But this had no real substance; all memory of life in Nazi Germany was lost to me, until…when did it take hold, the burden of guilt? Slowly, creeping in as I grew up—words whispered by the family about my father, my mother's bitter quarrels with Aunt Hedda, my longing for my lost sister. When it came, it was sudden—the bleak hours of a sleepless night—like ice in my heart, burning. Although I remembered no detail, I knew. Everything was changed.

Forgive me, but I thought I could tell you, I thought you might understand. Light floods the darkness, and for the first time I begin to see, to remember fragments of what happened. I don't know how to shut it all out any longer. Is this the beginning?

He read his letter through. It wouldn't do, a crazy confession to a person he'd met only once before. He tore it in half and started again.

Dear Miss Godwin,

I realise I want to tell you my story, as much of it as I can remember, if you are still willing to listen. How would you like to proceed?

The children he'd seen that day—the little slaves from Poland and Czechoslovakia—a miasma of decay hung round them. It had repelled and terrified him.

The letter to Leda Godwin slipped from his lap, the pen rolled away. He shivered, and looked up at the expanse of sky. The stars were difficult to make out in the orange glow of the city, but his eyes had adjusted to night, and he could see the slip of new moon above the metal railings that flanked the top of the buildings. In the distance a car door slammed and an engine revved, but the courtyard was silent. He could hear his own breath. He knew he should get up and go home. He put his head on his knees.

He was startled by the sound of footsteps over the stone flags and strained to look towards the alley. Miss Godwin. He recognised her dark figure against the light by the way she moved in her long coat, arms wrapped over her chest, head bowed. He thought to leave quickly, but there was nowhere to go without walking past her.

'Miss Godwin,' he called softly as she drew nearer. She stopped abruptly and saw him. It was odd the way she looked at him, longer than customary for people who scarcely knew each other.

'Miss Godwin,' he said again. 'Gregor Loeben.' He stood up.

'I know. I can see it's you.'

'I'm sorry. I was walking and I found myself here. I had your card in my pocket. I don't know why…I wanted to talk to you but…I wrote a note. I never expected you.'

'It's very late. I don't expect to find a man sitting in the yard so late at night.'

Was she humouring him? Her voice was toneless, her expression unreadable in the shadows. Desolation swept over him. It was the wrong thing to have done. He hadn't thought it through. Ruby always said he acted too much on impulse. He felt an urge to walk past her, without speaking, without looking back. Did he really want to tell anyone his story? What possible use could there be in doing that? Ruby was right. It was far too late, and long ago.

'It was foolish of me. I'm sorry to intrude on you.'

She hesitated before speaking.

'You might as well come in. Be careful though. It's a labyrinth inside.'

She unfastened the screen doors, unlocked an inner door, and he followed her into an empty space smelling of dust and tea. By the dim light of a naked bulb that hung from the ceiling, and, after that, the beam of a torch she took from her pocket, they climbed wooden stairs, walked along corridors, and steeper stairs until they reached the fifth floor. She unlocked another door and they entered a chilly space, divided by tarpaulins tied to the ceiling beams. There was the lingering smell of paraffin. She struck a match and held it to a gas lamp. The light flared up.

'I should explain. It wasn't planned or I would have telephoned you...'

'You've already explained,' she interrupted. 'I was expecting you anyway. It was unfortunate our meeting. It ended badly. But I knew you would come. Sit down.'

There were two wooden chairs by the window, with a small table between. The table held a neat pile of papers, a typewriter, and the gas lamp. He sat on the nearest chair, his hands folded, tense in his lap.

'Do you drink?' She reached for a bottle and two tumblers. 'I find it clears the mind. It's a kind of brandy.'

'Brandy would be very nice.'

She poured two large glasses and placed one beside him on the table. The other she held. She remained standing.

'Miss Godwin, I think I can help you with your theatre. There are things I've begun to remember.' He spoke in a rush, then stopped, brushed his hand over his face. He couldn't say more.

She waited a while before speaking. 'I've thought about you since our meeting,' she said. 'How should I presume to probe into your past?'

He darted a look at her, then away. His gaze glanced off the tarpaulin wall and back to his hands clasping the brandy glass.

'That's not what you said in the restaurant,' his voice caught in his throat. He swallowed. 'Nobody before has ever wanted to know anything.'

'I'm no psychiatrist. I use people for my own ends, not theirs.'

He turned the glass round and round slowly. I don't need a psychiatrist, he thought. 'It didn't seem so, the way you listened when I first told you I was German.'

'Most people are incapable of listening. I listen because I'm intensely curious. But my skill as a listener shouldn't be mistaken for kindness. I use people. Their stories are my raw material. I'm neither kind nor empathetic.'

'You talked of redemption that night,' he said. 'That sounds like great kindness to me.'

She smiled briefly.

'My work touches people for a moment. That's what I hope. But I have no grand illusions about it. It's just something I have to do.'

Silence fell between them. Neither moved nor spoke. He tried to make sense of what she said against the remembered image of her he'd held and pondered since they met.

'I don't believe you,' he said at last. 'You seem to me more serious about everything than that. You don't seem to me to be a frivolous person.'

'You have to understand, I'm exacting, difficult to please, and uncompromising. On the whole people find me exhausting and frustrating to work with.'

'Why do you try to put me off after searching me out for so long?'

'Because your cousin is right—I am no doctor.'

'I don't ask for a doctor. What do you think I am? I'm not sick.' He stopped abruptly, surprised by his anger. 'I will go then. I'm sorry.' He stood up.

It seemed to Gregor that she knew he wouldn't leave. She waited, motionless, her eyes lowered. He sat down again. She poured more brandy into both glasses.

'But theatre, its power to illuminate the truth, is at best nothing more than a flicker of light in the dark,' she said. 'Ultimately I work for myself; it's my struggle to make sense of the world. I'm driven. Horrific events have taken place this century. You survived the worst of it. I try to understand the truth beneath the events—elusive though that is. In another life I might have written history books.' She sat down opposite him. 'Your confession that day, the way it seemed to come out of nowhere, struck me—yes, I want to know everything. How could I not? But something holds me back.' Her voice faded and she sipped the brandy. 'A sense perhaps that I should take great care,' she said quietly.

'I make recordings of people's lives on this machine.' She pointed to a small cassette player on the bookshelf. 'It helps me to hear the voice as well as the story. The voice can reveal a lot.'

'What do you do with the cassettes when they're full of stories?'

'I listen over and over again, until my own words come, until I see where I want to go. Then I label and store them in a locked cupboard.'

'And the key to the cupboard?'

'I keep it safe. I shouldn't, like Bluebeard, tempt anyone with it.'

'Bluebeard? His wives, his cupboard of severed heads?'

'Yes.' She caught his eye and laughed briefly. 'Forgive the allusion. I always found that story oddly beguiling. What's really going on, what's the real meaning of it all?' She stood up again. 'I'll show you the rehearsal space. This is my living quarter.'

'You live here?'

'A few of us do—dancers, artists and writers. This entire floor is mine, but I don't stay here all the time. The rent is very low and we can work day and night, when we like.'

He followed her into a great empty space with windows on two sides.

'There's always something going on during the day, dance classes and rehearsals, which is why I often work at night. It's quieter.'

They walked round the edge of the room; she trained the torch up the walls into the crossed beams of the roof. They paused at a window and stood looking out over the river. A gleaming frost had formed.

'I don't like mornings. I can never work then. I walk around at night, when I think best.'

'I don't like mornings either.'

'What is your work?'

'You've seen it, Ruby plays the accordion, I move. Also, I look after the people who live with us in number 7. We have the rent they give us, and Ruby models for art classes. We're used to surviving on little.' It was strangely intimate standing at the edge of the big empty room with her. 'It seems as if only we are awake.'

'But that's not true. All over the city people are being born, dying, being conceived. The wandering insomniacs, the poets, the nurses and bankers.'

'The people calling out in pain.'

'Or ecstasy.'

'The drugged and the drunk.'

'The people whose hearts are broken. Tomorrow afternoon,' she said. 'Can you come here at three?'

'Who owns my story when it's recorded?'

She paused. He could hear her breathing.

'I think it finally becomes something that belongs to neither of us.'

'And then?'

'And then, who knows?'

On the other side of the river they watched two dark figures walk towards each other and stop to speak before passing by.

'How long have you followed me?'

'I first saw you on October 17th last year.'

'That long ago. I never saw you.'

'Why should you? I'm only one in a crowd. There you were—it was a beautiful afternoon—you were standing in the shadow of that block of flats at World's End, the bulldozers, the cranes, the workmen digging, and you looked so incongruously out of place, fragile, as if you might disappear if I looked away for a moment. The way you danced was mesmerising. That's what made me stop. I watched many times after that. Then the first thing you tell me is that you're German. The way you said it, that was the extraordinary thing.'

'Extraordinary?'

'Yes. Because of course, I knew.'

'How could you know?' He shivered.

'Just that when you told me, it made sense. I realised I'd known all along.'

'Was it you on the bridge, Miss Godwin, that night when the birds were flying.'

'Yes. And the girl who sang, and the boy by the edge of the water.'

'That was beautiful, wasn't it? Luminous. I wanted to say something to you then.'

He swayed with exhaustion. The light of dawn streaked the sky. He longed to go home, to sleep.

Gregor considered how to dress for his first interview with Leda Godwin. Meeting her required a particular image;

something understated—a white collarless shirt, pale linen suit, and the brogues he'd found in an antique market, and polished to a shine. Emerging from his room, he found Ruby sitting on the stairs gazing out of the long window.

'You look as if you're going for tea with an old English piano teacher,' she said.

'That's very specific.'

'Of course. I remember it well. When I first visited England I had a tartan dress with a lace collar. All those teas, and the ladies smelling of rose water. I had to sit so still and quiet whilst Mama talked. I hope Miss Godwin doesn't ask you to be quiet.'

Gregor smoothed the collar of his jacket and closed his eyes. He imagined walking into the sea, felt that floating sensation, his mind fading into the palest blue.

'You're scared.'

'No.'

'I don't believe you.'

'Scared isn't the right word.'

'To hell with the right word.'

'Let me go, Ruby.'

Gregor ran down the stairs past Willoughby Stone, who was wheeling his bike in from the street. 'Good evening my friend. Tomorrow I will cook. I promise that. A feast.'

Gregor loitered in front of the cake shop window. There were lemon tarts—Ruby's favourite, that rich buttery lemon curd and the lardy pastry. They were selling half price. Did that mean they were stale? Did Miss Godwin eat cakes? He shouldn't go empty handed. He bought two in a white card box tied with brown raffia.

He took a bus along the embankment, as far as the ruined church garden. As he got off, he thought there was someone watching him from the wall of the churchyard— the boy with the roses? When he turned again to look there was nobody. He shivered. *Who is it that walks always behind me?* He'd read that once in a poem.

He crossed the river to the wharf. He was early, of course—he was habitually too early or too late. He couldn't disturb Miss Godwin before she expected him, so he strolled down the street between the great warehouses, looking up at the gantries crossing from one building to another. The sun shone in diagonal shafts over the stone flags. Again he had the uncomfortable feeling he was being watched, and turned sharply. A cloud of tiny flies crossed his path, the air full of their vibrations. How odd, he thought, out of nowhere. Where had they come from and where would they go—lost, in another world, amongst the bricks and mortar of the city?

His heartbeat was fast and hard, his hands gripped the cardboard box with the lemon tarts. He looked up at Leda Godwin's window, thought he saw her and waved. Maybe there had been nobody watching him descend from the bus. Maybe the flies had never whirled by—trickery of the light.

It was chilly when the sun dipped. He checked the time. The door would be open, she'd said, and he must walk in. He tried to remember the way to the top floor by the intricate network of stairs and passageways, and felt his way in the half-light. There were no rehearsals yet. It was eerie and quiet. The scent of tea and spices hung in the dusty air.

Does she intend to disconcert me? Ruby is right—perhaps I shouldn't trust her. I can still leave. But he continued to climb to the top floor.

She stood against a window with its gridded square of sky, and turned to greet him. He thought at first that she wore the white coat of a medic, as if she prepared to operate on him. He wanted to run back down the labyrinth of stairs and far away. Instead he took another step into the room, and saw he'd been mistaken. The light had created a disturbing illusion. She wore a green dress. Her hair was plaited and wound close to her head.

'Good afternoon Miss Godwin. I've brought lemon curd tarts.' He looked around then placed the box on the desk. 'They're so delicious.'

She smiled. The clouds shifted and sunlight burned into the room. The tarpaulins created pockets of dark shadow, so the whole space was broken into dazzling light and shade.

'We can begin as soon I've prepared the recorder.'

Gregor's hands started to tremble; his throat was dry.

'I find I'm nervous. I so often talk to myself. But now, faced with you, with this machine, I'm afraid I might not remember anything. After all, I left Germany in 1946 when my Aunt Hedda rescued me and took me back to Holland. I returned for a few years with my mother when I was sixteen. I left for good when I was twenty. When the war was over my parents and sister seemed to have disappeared. Aunt Hedda and Ruby were the only relatives anyone could find. Ruby is my first cousin. My only cousin, I believe. I can't be absolutely certain of anything. There's very much I can't remember, you see. Maybe my father had a brother or sister. Maybe there are other cousins. But I don't think so.'

He went to the window and leant his forehead against the glass, feeling the warm sun on his face. He realised how agitated he was, chattering on, just like Ruby.

'With one touch the tape recorder will seem alive. My interrogator will enter the room.'

'There's no interrogator, I assure you.'

'It doesn't feel that way.'

Gregor paced, counting under his breath, ten steps from one window to the other. What flared into his mind, making him stop abruptly and stare at the floor, was the thought of Ruby's parents—of the night they were arrested by the Dutch Nazis.

He was startled by the touch of Leda's hand on his arm.

'Gregor. There's no need to do anything. You can leave now if you want to.'

'It's nothing. I thought of the Gestapo. It seemed so real for a moment. It's over now.'

She poured brandy into the coloured glasses and handed him one. He hesitated at the thought of brandy so early in the day.

'Purely medicinal,' she said, glancing at him.

'You can record now, Miss Godwin. I'll tell you everything I remember, but may I sit here, not at the desk?' He crouched against the wall, between the sun and shade, knees tucked up. 'I'm ready.'

At the click of the *record* and *play* buttons Gregor lifted his gaze from the floor. Leda adjusted the microphone and spoke.

Tape one: London April 1974, recording Gregor Loeben.

The whirr of the spools turning.

The first memories—the house in Essen and my childhood—it's like having a few pieces of a jigsaw and not being able to fit them together to make the whole picture. When I dream about the house, as I have these last few weeks, I discover so many doors and empty rooms, and it's much bigger than I thought. When I wake, I try to go back to make certain, but everything slips away again. How many doors led from the hall, which way did the staircase turn between the floors—there were three routes up I think. Where was the furniture placed in my bedroom? Yet I see Father's study and Mother's drawing room with crystal clarity.

In that house, where I was born, I had a place in the parlour where I could hide, tucked between the window and the heavy curtain. I would sit there and look far into the distance, over the vast waste of factories and steel forges. I would imagine the chimneys were a forest of ghostly trees and the furnaces were the wine bottles of giants. I would pretend the whole land was mine, I was a Baron of Steel, and the long laden trains and barges made their slow journeys at my command. At sunset the sky glowed red, as if on fire. I knew hell would be like that, the sky burning forever. I tasted metal in my mouth, and the hedges in the garden and the cabbages in the vegetable plot were coated in a dust of soot. Soot fell from the sky like black snow. But even in this dark place the birds sang. I'd run out and stand under the trees to listen, wondering at their mysterious language.

I can see the shadow of my father at night—a great black figure climbing the stairs. A life-size portrait of der Führer hung over the fireplace in the hall. Above the portrait hung a golden cross and chain, and the Nazi flag.

I will tell you about my family, Miss Godwin. The oldest was my grandmother on my father's side. She seemed ancient to me, though she can't have been older than seventy. Until she quarrelled with Mother, she lived with us in her own rooms full of dark shiny furniture, and paintings of flowers, fruit and ships on a stormy sea. My grandmother loved God, Hitler and my father. She often told me that God had sent der Führer to look after Germany, and for that reason all would be well. I do not care for your mother, she said. Your mother is unkind to me and I care for her no more than I do for that footstool. But through the greatness of God and Hitler, your mother's unkindness will be eclipsed. I knew even then it was a strange thing to say to a child.

My father and mother loved and hated each other in equal measure. Often my father would take meals alone in his study and I rarely saw him eat. I believed children needed food, in order to grow, but adults ate only for pleasure. My father was far too busy for pleasure. Sometimes I was allowed into his study where there was an imposing desk with a green-shaded lamp, and a bookcase that reached the ceiling. The room smelt strongly of something medicinal. Another portrait of Hitler hung behind the desk, and two smaller photographs on a table by the window showed him standing amidst a group of men wearing swastikas on their armbands, my father amongst them. Because of these photographs I knew that my father was an important man. I was very proud.

My mother was much talked about, not only because she rarely left the house, but also because she had once been very beautiful. She revered beauty and perfection. They were the highest measure. In her room everything had to be in the right place. She was quick to rage or to despair, to blame everyone but herself for her daily sufferings. I learned very early in life to be careful not to anger her, and always, even when I grew up and we lived together in England

and Holland, I tried not to upset the balance. When she was upset a cloud of misery would hang over us for days.

My sister, Mari-Louise, was eight years older than me. Our parents were preoccupied and inconsistent. Mother often shut herself in her room, and Father was doing important work, so we were very much left alone. Mari was like a mother as well as a sister to me.

Mari-Louise had beautiful red-gold hair and wore it plaited round her head, the way you do yours, Miss Godwin. Her skin was clear and pale and her eyes blue-grey. She was, our grandmother said, a flawless Aryan maiden if you looked at the right side of her face. But nature was cruel. On the left was her Imperfection—a red birthmark that extended over her left cheek and to the corner of her eye.

Grandmother regularly announced how Mari's mark was formed in the shape of the map of the Germany in the days of the Weimar Republic. But this was no consolation for my mother who said the child was flawed and her beauty marred. I liked her birthmark. When she lay beside me, after I'd woken with bad dreams, I would trace my finger over her cheek, which made her smile because it tickled her like an insect crawling.

Sometimes now, when I wake in the night, I forget I'm in London. I think I'm back in my room in Germany. I see the rocking horse by the fireplace, and my shelf of rocks and the chess set, and I'm sure Mari is in her room next door. I call for her and hear her soft footsteps outside, her sigh, and the turn of the doorknob. She was always with me, the soft warmth of her hand close to my face as we walked in the snow, her furry gloves stroking my skin.

Then with a sick feeling, I know it's over and I'll never see her again. I don't even have a photograph. How could I? Everything has gone. An awful thought comes—perhaps she never existed at all. I fight for breath. Did I invent her because I so wanted an older sister? At the same time I know that's irrational, a wretched game my mind taunts me with. Aunt Hedda would testify that Mari was born in 1929, and was the sweetest little girl. Hedda grieved that she never saw her again when she left Germany in 1933.

I try to reach my beloved sister, to call her back, and it's as if I'm the one locked up in death. I want to escape from my body, from the

61

world. It's as if fragments of memory, of my childhood, fly like birds in the night towards me, and then off into the dark again. But my sister shines out. She was the heart of everything. Is it her story I'm telling? Will the telling bring her back? Where is she?

The spools of the cassette turned. Gregor closed his eyes and tapped his fingers on the floor, as if marking out a tune on the piano.

'Do you want to stop?' Leda asked.

He shook his head and sighed.

I know this too, for certain—as a child I believed there were three fathers.

'Tell me what you mean by three fathers. I think I understand, but tell me anyway.'

The first father was my biological father. His face would shift, as if he switched his mask from kind to utterly cold and distant, so we never knew how he'd be from day to day, or what he really was. The second father was Adolf Hitler, who was said to look after and protect all German people, even the grown ups, as if they too were children. We called him der Führer. I would think of him when I lay alone in bed unable to sleep because my mother and father had quarrelled. Although der Führer was absent he was always in my heart. The third father was more abstract. My grandmother talked of him often. Ah, his face is terrible, she would say, and I imagined a great ghostly face looming out of the darkness—a mouth that opened wide, like the mouth of a whale, to swallow me. You will see Almighty God when you die, and for that reason you must pray with all your heart for your sins to be forgiven. I didn't know what my sins were.

There was that day, the day I came face to face with Hitler, although I see mere flashes as if in a dream—a castle with a lake, the car that drove us there, and great crowds of people waving flags. It was after that day that my father and Hitler became confused in my mind. The two became one. That day he bent down and spoke to me, and smiled with a strange light. I can still see his eyes; they were blue, intensely focused.

'Hitler?'

'Yes, Hitler, who else?'

June 1941 Germany

Mari-Louise scrubbed Gregor's face and ears, clipped his hair neatly to his head and helped him dress in his best clothes. He had soft leather lederhosen, a cap with a blue jay's feather, and braces embroidered with edelweiss. On his arm he wore a band with the swastika—truly a little German boy.

Down in town gleaming tanks, like monsters, rolled by in grand procession, rank on rank of soldiers marched in their uniforms and shining boots, and the band played upbeat tunes that made Gregor skip with delight. The sun beat down on the people lining the streets, so the sweat beaded their faces—factory workers and managers, with their wives and children, dressed in their best clothes, shop keepers, doctors and priests. Everyone smiled and cheered. *Der Führer is coming. He is coming at last.* A sea of flags waved, and arms stretched proud in salute. Gregor's chest was tight to bursting.

They went by car to the Villa Hügel, driving slowly past the crowds. He held Mari's hand, looked out at the faces and felt he must be a very important person too. Some people smiled, others stared. So many eyes, looking at him.

In the great marble hall, scented with lilies and thick with cigar smoke, ladies fanned their faces and sipped tea. Old men in grey uniforms stood firm and attentive under family portraits, and other important men, like his father, stood waiting for the Moment of Arrival.

It was Gregor's turn to dance a waltz with his partner. She was a rosy girl with fat damp fingers. Afterwards they could eat ice cream, but before ice cream was allowed, the girl led him onto the polished floor with the other children. As she whirled him round he caught sight of a ghostly little boy in the mirrors and froze, but she shoved him into place and, huffing and puffing, she pulled him up and down the polished floor to the music. The ladies laughed. Shamed, he ran to Mari and buried his face in her lap.

Gregor knew his father's heavy footfall, even though he still snuggled into Mari. His father's hand engulfed his own, and squeezed so tight that Gregor couldn't wriggle. He was prised away from his sister and led through the glass doors onto the terrace. He's angry with me. I spoilt it all and will be punished. Gregor's breath came in little bursts. His father said nothing. He took him down the steps into the meadow. He will beat me when we're alone.

The pollen rose in clouds and tiny butterflies, blue, white, yellow, fluttered in the billowing grass. Gregor was too sick in his stomach to enjoy them. The day had taken on that metallic electric sensation that came sometimes, making everything tinny and distant.

A lady stood on the shore of the lake. She waved her white-laced hand and they walked to meet her. Ernst—she called out his father's name. Gregor had never seen anyone so beautiful, her radiant smile and golden hair pinned up with a white rose and glittering diamonds. When she bent to kiss him, her soft lips brushed his forehead, and he caught the sweetness of her perfume.

'So Gregor—what a big boy you are. Have you been good?'

With a heavy heart he shook his head.

'Ah, I believe you've been very good,' she said, looking up at his father. 'He's so like you Ernst, he's yours, all yours, a perfect fledgling Nazi.'

His father placed his hand on Gregor's head and ruffled his hair. In the distance the band played and Gregor felt faint with relief. It was going to be all right after all. He ran ahead to pick long stemmed daisies for the lady.

'Such a sweet little boy.'

His father lifted Gregor and swung him high so his head brushed against the leaves of the willow trees. He dropped his fistful of daisies, and flies battered his face. Then he was lowered to the ground and set on his feet.

'Run along ahead and hide,' his father said. 'I'll catch you soon.'

Gregor found a place by the edge of the lake between two fallen branches, and crouched down. It was a good place and he waited, anticipating his father's praise at how clever he was to hide so well. When nobody came he crept out and parted the silvery reeds. He saw his father under the willow trees. His body was pressed against the woman, his hand tangled in her hair that had come undone. He seemed to be eating the woman's face. Gregor watched more carefully. No, it was kissing. His stomach lurched and his heart beat hard. He wanted to watch, but knew he mustn't. It was private and he felt ashamed. He wanted to be with them, but knew he wouldn't be wanted. Burning with shame, Gregor left his hiding place and staggered, fast as he could, back to the villa.

The children he'd danced with stood hand in hand in a long line on the garden terrace. The girl who'd been his partner stepped forward and pulled him into line. 'Wait,' she whispered. 'He is coming.'

Gregor had no idea who she meant. He could see only the important men in their uniforms. He stood, feet together, hands by his sides, and craned his neck to look.

'Der Führer.' The children nudged each other, whispered and stood tall with their chests stuck out. Gregor's heart seemed to turn over, for there indeed was Der Führer walking towards them. He passed along the line, smiling and bending over each child, patting heads and touching cheeks. Gregor wanted to run and stay at the same time. Perhaps der Führer was giving sweets? He anticipated the sweet, what it would smell and taste like? Then der Führer was beside him, his face at Gregor's level. Gregor wanted to back away from the stench that came from his mouth. For a second he held his breath and looked into Hitler's eyes, saw the reflected sky and the window of the villa. Then something happened. He was falling deeper and deeper. He couldn't take his gaze away. This was the look of love. Der Führer was gazing at him, Gregor von Loeben, with love. Gregor trembled with the knowledge that he was the chosen child.

'Stop recording, please.'

Leda pressed the *pause* button. Gregor got to his feet and went to the window. He opened the casement, and leant against the frame. Cool air entered the room. Outside someone wheeled a bicycle across the street and called out good-afternoon.

'It's like a curse.' He shook his head, rubbed his hand over his eyes. 'Do you ever feel you're being watched? That beautiful boy with the roses in the restaurant—I keep wondering how he knew I was German.'

'I don't believe he did. He was just trying to amuse us and totally failing. He might as well have thought all three of us were German.'

'That's what Ruby says. So often I feel I'm being watched, that someone has been sent to report back to a higher authority. They're searching for me in lieu of the father, who was never caught, and I'm called on to atone. I know it's improbable, but at the same time I'm certain it's true. And now they will have this recording.'

'I promise you, Gregor, that nobody will ever hear this without your consent. Let's continue. Can you?'

He sat down at the desk.

'There's something else,' he said. 'I'm sure that afternoon was the first time I saw the beautiful woman with my father. She was truly lovely, an ideal—I saw her the way one only really sees as a child. She wasn't merely another human being, like me, but somehow elevated. I gave her a name, Angelia, or Angel. I had the terrible notion my father had devoured her.'

Leda glanced at him and pressed the *record* button again.

As I said before, my father had two faces—one was arrestingly sweet, the other suspicious and cold. The coldness concentrated into a hard knot that appeared between his narrowed eyes. His feet in those shining black boots turned out and struck the ground with pent up violence.

When he was kind, life was kind. I longed then to grow up like him. He was so handsome—my tall, fair father. On his sweet days he would kiss me. He was a Nazi, yes, but as far as I knew there was no other way to be. My Aunt Hedda had fled to Holland as soon as Hitler came to power, and my grandfather, who was vociferously anti-Nazi, had died. By the time I was born there was no other reality. Germany was the Greatest Nation, and Hitler had risen from obscurity to save us.

One day I remember very clearly—I was called to my father's room. I opened the door quietly and crept in. There was a smell, not exactly perfume, more medical, maybe alcoholic, I don't know. I've never smelt it since. I would know instantly if I did because it made me feel deeply melancholic, despair washed over me. My father was staring into space, his fingertips touching. The red veins in his cheeks stood out. When he turned to look at me, it was as if he'd only just noticed I was there, and he laughed. I didn't understand what was funny.

My father got up, knelt beside me and took my hands. His voice was intense and whispery. I'd never heard him speak like that before. His blue eyes shone, like glass.

We have laid the path, he said. All hope lies before you, and the new world will be yours—all the wonder and glory of it. My son, my beloved son. I feel such joy. He pressed my face to his chest so forcefully I had to twist my head to breathe. I looked down at the shininess of his boots, and the crease he'd made when he walked, and I thought one day someone would invent boots that didn't crease with our bending toes. An odd thought to have at that moment, with my face crushed between his arm and chest, but I was scared. It seemed even then that the normal order of things was unbalanced and everything was precarious.

We knelt together on the parquet floor and said a prayer. Our Father...only it wasn't the Lord's Prayer. It would translate something like this—Führer, my Führer, given me by God, protect and preserve my life…I can't go on. It was the prayer of the Hitler Youth. He said each line first, and made me repeat it after him. He asked was I strong, and I told him I didn't know. He said I must work on being very strong, like a warrior.

After that I was obsessed. I drank the cream of the milk whenever I could find it, and I lifted rocks round the gardens, making patterns with them and then moving them again, trying to carry more than one at a time. Holding my breath, I made dances with my feet and hands to see how long I could go without breathing. I ran round the garden and hung upside down on trees. But I was never called to my father's room again. I was sad because I had no chance to show him how strong I'd become.

My grandmother said Hitler's eyes shone with God's great love. She'd met him only once, but she felt he'd seen into her soul, and her life was changed from that moment. My grandmother kissed her golden crucifix and hung it over his portrait. Almighty God gave the German people the gift of Adolf Hitler. He was sent to save us all, to make us a great nation.

This is how it was, Miss Godwin. I'm telling you these things even though they stick in my throat, because you'll understand the times we were living in, and how low we had sunk. As a child I was in earnest. I'm ashamed of the child I was, and at the same time I pity him. I believed in Der Führer, with all my heart. And for that reason I'm haunted and see no end to it.

Leda turned off the recorder.

'We'll stop now, for today. You're exhausted. Me too. I'll make tea, unless you want more brandy. Or brandy and tea?'

She smiled. She had an aura of calm about her, as if she'd been told many terrible things, but nothing would shock or perturb her.

'What can I do for you in return for this?'

'But you're the one who's giving. Don't you see that?'

On a Saturday in April Ruby and Willoughby left the house before sunrise, without planning a destination.

'A mystery walk,' Ruby said. 'Just to see where chance will take us.'

At each street corner they took turns to decide which way to go, though Ruby insisted they took the unfamiliar routes—better that way.

'I followed a stray dog once,' she said. 'I ended up quite lost. Dogs have funny ideas about where to go, essentially rubbish bins and car parks.'

As they walked the sky grew lighter, the birds sang. The newsagents drew up the shutters and opened their doors. The florist brought buckets of orange and white tulips into the street, and glanced up as they passed—a woman in a long red coat with a cloth bird pinned to her hat, and a dark-haired slender young man, slightly round-shouldered.

'I was married once,' Ruby said. She had already told him this, but he didn't seem to have heard. A bus was passing at the time, which was perhaps why—though he was often like that, reticent, slow to respond, out of shyness or reserve, she didn't know. 'That's how I first came to live in England. He was English.'

'What happened?' Willoughby had heard her the first time, and not known what to say, though there was no need to say anything at all. Ruby would talk.

'I met him at a party we had in Amsterdam for my mother's sixtieth birthday. I knew he was watching me. He walked across the crowded room. Is it you, he said, and looked at me with such a profound and keen expression even I was amazed. Nobody had ever said anything like that to me before. So I said, yes. Yes, it's me. Here I am! A week later he asked me to marry him.'

'Didn't you even think about it?'

'Only for a moment. How could I have said no? The story would be over before it began, and I'd never know the end. So we got married, and we were quite happy for a while. But you're right, I should have thought a bit longer, because after a few months I turned out not to be The One after all. Instead I was a Great Big Disappointment. I tried not to mind too much. He walked out and I stayed in England anyway. Then my mother's friend left the Gladstone Terrace house to me, and Gregor came, and you see, everything turned out fine. It always does, don't you find?'

When Willoughby retraced their steps later in his mind, he remembered where they'd been at each point in Ruby's story. In his sketchbook he drew a map so he would always remember that morning. They were walking alongside a beech hedge just coming into leaf, when she told him about her marriage. He noticed a Mint Aero chocolate wrapper was caught on the twigs. The sun lit up the side of her face as she turned to him. He wanted to keep looking. He didn't want her to know that.

'Do you want children Willo?' She didn't wait for his answer. 'You'd be a good father. I'd be a hopeless mother.' She looked into the distance. 'I'm so glad we never had one. I'd be sure to leave the pram in the park and forget until I was home—what a disaster that would be. But maybe for Gregor it would be nice.'

It was always Gregor.

'But I'll never marry again, or have children.'

They were passing a row of telephone boxes. He thought of how she had kissed him the afternoon she'd first seen his drawings, and how, for a long time afterwards, he still felt the imprint of her lips on his.

'We have the same birthday, Gregor and me. Isn't that a coincidence? Gregor was born on 22nd January 1936 in Germany, and I was born exactly eight years later, a month earlier than I should have been, lucky to be born at all.'

'You told me that.'

'Did I?'

'Yes, the very first time we met.'

'Sorry. I'm hopelessly forgetful. The first thing I remember as a baby is being pushed in my perambulator into the forest. I remember the pattern of light and shade as the leaves moved in the wind, and my mother's face looking down at me. I didn't know Gregor then. Are you listening, Willo? I'm not boring you, am I?'

He smiled and shook his head.

'Gregor arrived from Germany after the war. My mother went to fetch him because they thought the rest of his family had gone. I was a toddler, and he seemed grown up to me, even though he was only a boy. He came with a little suitcase. Inside it was a pair of socks, a torn shirt, a pair of shorts, a blanket, and a wooden soldier with the paint all chipped. That's the story Aunt Marianne told me. Gregor can't remember anything. At least he couldn't until he met Leda Godwin—God help us!

'He never left my side. Aunt Marianne said I was always crawling and running around with Gregor chasing me. We'd explore the underneath of things, and hide from the grown ups. I would tickle his face and make him laugh. Everyone was glad when Gregor laughed. They all tried so hard to be happy, to forget. Oh life! We still rejoice when he laughs, of course. It's a rare pleasure.

'It snowed one winter. We sat together in the window seat and watched the snowflakes swirling through the trees. My mother came in, silently, the way she did, put her arms round us both and sang a fragment of music. It seemed so magical, the three of us and the sad song.'

Ruby stood in the middle of the pavement, lost for a moment. Willoughby touched her hand.

'I'm hungry now,' he said. 'Shall we find breakfast?'

'Oh yes, excellent. I'm ravenous.'

There was a café in the next street. They ordered eggs and toast and sat in the window. A radio played, and there was the sound and smell of food frying. Ruby gazed at Willoughby over her mug.

'I love Gregor, you see.'

'I know.'

'Do you? I suppose you must. I do talk rather a lot, I know. It's a very odd kind of love, because sometimes he makes me mad. It's not how I feel about anyone else.'

'Even the English husband?'

'Oh him. I try not to think too much about that. I've had lots of boyfriends since because I like to be admired and sex is such fun, isn't it, don't you think?'

'Fun!' he laughed.

She looked at him in surprise.

'I'm sorry. You say the weirdest things at times.'

'Well, it's possibly the nicest way I can think of to pass the time.' She shrugged. 'I open my mouth before I think, so they say. I thought for a while it would be nice if we were lovers. But you're so kind and thoughtful, and I'm really not. What do you think?'

Willoughby looked down at the yellow plastic table, moved the toast crumbs into a pile with his finger. He felt his cheeks colouring.

'Does Gregor love you?' he asked.

'Love me. Who knows? He loves everyone. Also Gregor is in the middle of himself, if you know what I mean, trapped in his obsessive nightmare.'

A bus went by, briefly blocking the sunlight. When it passed and Willoughby looked up, he saw a cat balancing along the railings across the road. A lucky black cat. A bubble of happiness burst inside him. He smiled, and turned to look her full in the face. Her eyes were dark and flecked with gold, full of light and depth. He'd never quite dared to look before.

'Why are you smiling?'

'I don't know. It all seems funny—me living in your house, you and Gregor, the others. It's not as I expected.'

'You see, we're bound together, Gregor and me, part of the same thing, our family, all the things that happened. I don't know how to be without him, but I so long to be free sometimes, Willoughby. That's probably why I got married.' She laughed, unexpectedly, as if catching his happiness.

Afterwards he wished he'd answered her question, but she seemed to forget she'd asked it, and it was too late.

Gregor wandered past the school where Willoughby Stone was caretaker, but he didn't see Willoughby stop in the yard and wave, or hear his name called. Since the first interview with Leda, he'd become obsessed with the idea that there had been a woman with his father on the day they'd met Hitler, and that he'd seen this woman again, more than once. But there was also the beautiful girl he'd created in his mind, the one he called Angelia. The two had merged into one person, who was entirely beautiful and good.

In the French delicatessen he chose cheeses and pates, expensive luxuries he rarely bought. He let himself into the house and went upstairs to the drawing room where he heard Ruby playing a record. Ella Fitzgerald was singing, and Ruby lay on her back on the *chaise*, her arms dangling over her head, singing in harmony. She was dressed in a green satin gown, stretched tight over her rounded tummy and hips, and her hair was loose and tangled round her face. She had gold bangles on her wrists. Seeing him, she rolled over and sat up.

'What are you doing, creeping in on me?'

'I didn't creep, I didn't mean...'

She jumped up and put her arms round his neck. The bangles slid up her arms.

'It doesn't matter. I'm glad to see you. I've been so bored here on my own. Everyone is out except Moonlight, and I got tired with her prancing about fiddling with things in my room, so she's gone off to sulk.'

'You're dressed up.'

'Why not? If I don't wear my gowns here, where can I? Not out in the street. Anyway, this is how they want me to dress, the artists, when I sit later—they're all hopeless romantics. I must either be undressed, or dressed to the nines. And I'm going for dinner afterwards.'

'Where?'

'Oh I don't know. David Clare is taking me. Don't look at me like that. I make him happy, and he, in turn, buys me a good dinner.'

'I'm not looking like anything at you, Ruby.'

A bunch of orange blossom lay on the table beside her. She reached over and broke off a few of the creamy, sweet-scented flowers.

'I stole them from the park.' She held them to her face. 'What do you think? Pretty? I think I'll pin them in my hair. What's the matter? You look as if you've seen a ghost?'

'It's nothing. I don't know.'

There had been a woman with a flower in her hair that day when he met der Führer. He'd been right when he told Leda Godwin. But he'd met her again, more than once. He remembered her laughter when she looked up at his father, a small white hand with a blue sapphire ring, a slight scent of roses despite the falling snow—later a glimpse of her in the garden. Then nothing—as if she'd never existed. He touched the blossoms on the table. The petals were soft, wilted. He saw Ruby watching him.

'It's very pretty, yes. I bought things, Ruby.' He'd put the bag down somewhere on the way to the living room. 'We'll all have a feast later on. When are the others back?'

'I've no idea when they're back. I'm not their keeper,' she said, irritated. 'But remember, I'm not in. I'm going out with David.'

Gregor wandered out to look for his shopping, then forgot, and sat on the stairs, looking from the window at the tree. So often these days something would happen to spark his memory—like Ruby with the flower in her hair. Why had she picked orange blossom and decided to wear it? As if she knew his mind? She was singing again now, but her voice was different. She always sang differently when she knew he was unsettled—loud and resolutely cheerful.

The woman with the flower had said he was a dear little Nazi boy. Her eyes were silky with love. He had always wanted to be good, and when she looked at him like that, the sense of his own goodness suffused everything. But it was fleeting, lost in a moment if he woke in the night with a wet bed, or messed his shirt when eating—when his grandmother glared at him and said he was a bad child.

Then there was his fantasy Angelia. He'd lain sleepless in the dark and created stories about her. Angelia had been forced by an evil king to live in labyrinthine caves under the mountains, but Gregor bravely carried a lantern and went in search of her. He came to the edge of a tempestuous underground sea, and found her, half drowned, her hair floating round her. He threw himself in the waves and grasped her hand. With small variations, he played this scene many times. His love for her was warm, happy. Gregor likened it to shining a torch in a dark forgotten room. But Angelia wasn't real, whereas he knew the woman with the flower in her hair had been. She'd met him once from school and taken him to the café. He'd had chocolate, and sat close to her on the soft chair whilst his father went off to his important business. She'd said she would take him out again, the next week, and the one after. But she never did. He'd spent mornings gazing through the window from his perch behind the curtain, but nobody came down the road. Undaunted, he waited, certain she would come. He ran to the window to watch whenever he could.

One morning, he saw her walking away from the house towards the gate. She wore a pale yellow dress with pink and white ribbons in her hair. By the time he'd rushed out she was gone. There was no trace of her in the garden, or on the street. The leaves moved in the wind, seeds whirled down in a cloud, and the birds sang, but the garden was empty.

He leant his forehead against the fir tree. He couldn't bear it that she'd visited the house and hadn't come to see him. His mouth opened to cry, but he held his breath and no sound came. Gasping, he thumped his head three times on the trunk, grazing his skin on the bark. He couldn't be certain—maybe she had looked for him. The house was so big. Maybe she'd gone away, sad not to see him. He knew he must ask his father who she was, where she lived, and for permission to visit her. He needed to be bold. It was best to go before his courage failed him, so he went down to his father's study, knocked on the door and burst in.

'Father, I beg your pardon for disturbing you. Who is the lady with the rose, where does she live?'

His father looked up from his desk. His face seemed to merge with the map of Germany on the wall behind him, of all the countries that had become Germany. Everything blurred—the desk, the gold pen, the photograph of the smiling Führer.

'What are you talking about?'

Gregor tried to explain—his tongue felt thick and the words muddled.

'There is no such person.' His father's voice was cold.

'But there is, there was. She said I was a perfect Nazi boy. I gave her flowers, and then I hid and saw you with her. You walked by the lake, I saw you kissing her.'

His father got up from his desk. His hands dug into Gregor's shoulders and his face was as close as der Führer's face had been that lovely afternoon. He shook Gregor fiercely until his head felt loose and woolly.

'Come to, come to. I'm sorry, my son, but I have no idea who you are talking of. The day I remember, of course, but there was no woman, I can assure you.'

He smiled, but only with his lips.

Gregor closed his eyes, too stunned to cry. How could his father forget? One of us must be wrong. Both things can't be true. He had the sensation of falling, spiralling into a black hole, nothing to hold onto.

Gregor had displeased his father. He knew that because his father wouldn't turn his head to look down at him, and his feet were cruel in their shiny boots, stamping along the terrace. It was often that way. There were many times when he displeased his father profoundly.

He came to with a jolt. Where am I? Through the window the tree, bright with new buds, stood against the grey sky. London. I'm in London, of course. God help me.

'What's wrong?' Moonlight stood looking down at him. Dressed in a leotard, tights and a net ballet skirt, she seemed very tall. She knelt. 'You fell over. It's good I found you. Are you ill, Mr Loeben?'

He felt too exhausted to answer. He reached out his hand. She took it, and then bent her head to his chest.

'I can hear your heart. You are alive still, but it's beating very fast. Shall I help you to your room?'

He let her help him upstairs. He stretched out on his bed, floored by the wave of grief. It would pass. He just had to keep breathing, hard and fierce. Like any pain, it would pass.

Rain spattered the glass and trickled down. A tiny plane moved across the sky. Moonlight sat at the end of his mattress, looking down at him.

'You must rest,' she whispered, her pale face clouded with tragedy.

I'm remembering more now—the more I sit here with you, the more comes to light, Miss Godwin.

I'm thinking about my mother. Like father, she was volatile. From day to day Mari and I were unable to anticipate her moods, and there was no warning of change. It could be like this one moment, like this the other. Hopeless melancholia would descend; at first she'd pace round her room and shout to my father or grandmother, even though they weren't there, and then she'd cry, or refuse to speak at all. I used to think if only I could love her enough I'd be able to make her happy. But I didn't know how. I could never give the enormous love her heart longed for.

My mother, Gitta von Loeben, was slender, pale and spectral. She was beautiful, graceful like a dancer until the end of her life, and she needed lovely things around her. I'm trying to remember her room, to recall where everything was when we were called up to visit her on good days.

It was a light room with a window onto the garden, so the valley of smoking chimneys was hidden in the summer by a screen of shimmering leaves. Paintings of flowers hung on every wall. I used to gaze at one particular painting—two bright exotic birds with long tail feathers, amongst the orange lilies—I thought it was so beautiful. There were peacocks embroidered on silk, cut glass vases of roses, and gilded mirrors from floor to ceiling, so if I stood in a certain position I could see everything, including myself, reflected into infinity. Everything had to be dusted and in correct order. My mother was unsettled by disorder.

One night, when father and mother were quarrelling, and that happened often, I heard my father say, you throw yourself at me Gitta, like a parasite. There's something hideous about your craving. His voice was cold, almost toneless. He'd stopped shouting. I didn't fully understand, but I knew that for her it was terribly wounding. He left the room, walked past without seeing me.

I stood outside her door listening to the thin whine that rose and fell. I couldn't be sure it was her making such an eerie sound. Could it be the wind, or an animal in pain that had crawled through the open window into her room and couldn't get out? Horrified and fascinated at the same time, I opened the door a tiny crack and, peering in, saw her hunched on a chair by the window.

She was wearing a long white gown, her hair loose over her shoulders. On her feet were the slippers I liked to stroke because they were made of soft white feathers. A heavy smell of sweat, face powder and decaying flowers filled the room. Mother muttered to herself, and the words tailed off in a long low moan. She rocked backwards and forwards, her hands pressed between her thighs. Permit me to weep, at least, since you've abandoned me in this hell of your making, she said. I realised she was speaking to Father, although he'd left the room. I called out, Mummy. She stared, but didn't appear to see me. It's all right, it's me, I said. I ran into the room and stood, feet planted wide, facing her. Everything is all right.

Nothing here is all right. Tonight I will pack a few belongings and walk from this house forever. I will take a train far away where he'll never find me.

Don't go Mummy.

I put my arms round her and kissed her cheeks, over and over again as she cried.

My little boy, she said at last. *What will become of me?*

It will be all right. Everything is safe. Only words, but I had to make her believe them. *Shall I brush your hair?* I asked, although the hair brushing repulsed me. But I would do anything that day to make her happy.

I picked up the brush, stared at the embroidered flowers on the back, petals of white and pink and blue with yellow centres, so pretty. I lifted the brush to her hair. But when the bristles touched her head, she flinched, and pushed me away. *Leave me alone.* Her voice was harsh and aggressive.

I dropped the brush and left the room, as if struck by electricity. I ran down the stairs into the hall, and stood, facing the wall. My whole body shook.

By the time Mari found me I was frozen to the spot. Gently she turned me to look at her. She stroked my head until I could breathe properly again.

Our Grandmother had a small yellow bird in a cage hanging from the ceiling of her room. One summer day, when the window was open, another bird got in somehow, a wild brown bird from the garden. It fluttered desperately, battering against the glass to get out again, and flew around the room into the bars of the canary. For a moment everything seemed to be a whirl of beating wings and feathers. My grandmother screamed for someone to get the wild bird out, and covered her face with her hands. The door opened, and into this scene of chaos and confusion walked a young woman. I'd never met her before. It was a startling thing for a stranger to come into the house and Grandmother stopped her screaming in astonishment. The woman scooped up the bird, took it to the open window and let it fly off to freedom. Then she stood, hands on her hips, and looked directly at Grandmother. *Why do you keep a caged canary if you're afraid of birds?* she said.

Who are you, Grandmother asked? *Johanne Kuhn*, the woman replied.

Johanne Kuhn, twenty years old, bold and brave. She was hired as my nanny, and companion for Mari-Louise. Small and muscular, she had a fair, wind-chapped complexion, and curly red-gold hair that stuck out round her face. She was always active, restless, strong and determined with everything she did. Her small supple hands with those blunt fingers—they were always warm, and she would hold mine firmly, in a way that made me feel safe. She smelt of warm yeast, a good smell.

After the bird incident, Mari sobbed. I'm like the trapped canary, she said. I can't escape. And when the wild bird comes to free me, it's still no good, there's no way out. Johanne drew her chair up and wrapped her arms round her. Don't cry, my pet, my little love. It's cruel to keep birds in cages. Birds should be free. I would open the cage for him, but then your grandmother would send me away. But one day, we'll let him go. I promise, one day, when she's gone. Mari wept uncontrollably.

At that moment the evening sun poured through the windows, flooding the room with light, and it seemed like an auger, as if everything indeed might change for the better. We loved her, Johanne Kuhn. We loved her so much; she brought us a brief spell of happiness.

The Great Hope for Germany meant nothing in any real way to me through my infancy. It was the ground I sprang from and naturally believed in, but even though I tried so hard to become the strong Nazi boy, it was like acting a part in a bad play. What Mari and I felt most keenly, was our bleak and oppressive family life. Both parents fell far short of Hitler's archetype of the warrior father and the all-loving mother. But Mari adored Johanne. When Johanne came to live with us Mari changed from a timid girl, hiding her birthmark under a sweep of hair, to my courageous and beautiful sister. And for a spell she seemed so happy, quick to play and to giggle in ways I'd never seen.

But Johanne Kuhn brought more than this. She made us see Hitler's Third Reich in a new terrible light.

Gregor stopped speaking. Outside, the rain fell, and raindrops trickled down the pane, gathering speed as they met. Stillness settled over him, a weariness he often felt these days, as if he could stare into space with such intensity he would become the air itself. Leda watched him, waited. He blinked, rubbed his eyes.

Leda had arranged pebbles on the windowsill. He reached for one, took it and held it in his palm, felt the smooth coolness of it. He put his tongue to it. As a little child he'd collected stones, pieces of coal, flint and quartz. He'd always longed for a fossil. He used to search in the garden for them.

One afternoon the fog had lain damp and grey over the valley of factories, and they were confined in the house. Johanne, always restless, paced to the window to check the weather, opened books at random to read a few words before putting them down.

'It's really too bad this rain,' she said. She took Gregor's box of stones from the shelf. 'Let's sort them into colours and sizes. Yes, Gregor?' She tipped them onto the table.

Gregor perched on a chair beside her. He watched her as her fingers traced each facet of the rock. She bit her lip with concentration, as if she searched for something.

'What are you looking for?'

'Look carefully and you'll see creatures in this rock, little fish, ancient shrimps and eels. You do have a fossil after all. You've just never looked hard enough.'

'Let me look now.' He grabbed the rock from her and held it up to the light. But he couldn't see what she meant. He moved it away a little, stared and blinked.

'Surely you must be half blind and nobody has noticed and done anything about it. I'll tell the parents.' Her eyes glittered as she teased.

'I'm not blind. I see everything very well.'

'You're blind as a mole.'

He pounded her with his fists. She laughed and caught his wrists to stop him.

'There, I'm still stronger than you.'

Her face was so close he could feel her breath on his cheeks.

'You look a bit like a monkey,' he said. 'A monkey with curly hair.'

'Well that's a nice thing to say! What do you think Mari-Louise?'

Mari looked up from her book and smiled.

'You're much nicer than a monkey.'

'But I only said monkey because they have a smiling look in their faces, and you have that, Johanne. Monkeys are clever too.'

Whilst she considered that, he sprang out of her grip. She laughed.

'There, you won with cunning. Now sit down, be quiet and look at that rock again until you see the ancient sea creatures. Give me some peace.'

Johanne couldn't keep quiet for long.

'I do actually see people as animals,' she said, lowering her voice. 'Only you must never tell anyone. The adults would say it's not respectful. If you were an animal what would you be, I wonder?' She looked at Gregor, her head on one side. 'Maybe a little grey mouse.'

'What am I?' Mari asked. 'Tell me what you see.'

'A graceful pony, and I'm a horse, a strong old workhorse.'

'Strong and wise.'

'Are horses wise?'

'Maybe not, but if you were a horse you would be.'

Johanne glanced at the door to make sure nobody was coming. 'You'll never guess what animal I think Adolf Hitler is,' she whispered. Her eyes shone with mischief.

Mari pondered, her hand to her mouth.

'Maybe a lion?'

'A lion. I'm sure that's what most people think he is. But I see Herr Hitler as nothing more than a rat.'

'But a rat would never be able to lead Germany.' Mari looked at her, wide eyed.

'The rat in my head can, at least whilst its luck holds out. I see a big fat vicious rat. I had a bad dream of being chased by one once. That's how I know how nasty they are.'

Johanne reached for a pencil and drew a rat in a Nazi uniform, with a face that looked like Hitler's. She added a long tail, protruding teeth and a rat-hand extended in salute.

Gregor felt tightness in his chest. He took a breath and something seemed to explode inside him—everything falling, broken into fragments.

'Yes, I see, I see.' He hopped around the room, wildly. 'Der Führer, der Führer,' he sang in a high-pitched voice.

'Gregor, stop. You're out of control.' Johanne caught hold of him and pulled him onto her lap. He wriggled but she held him tight, until all the madness fell out of him again.

Mari picked up the drawing.

'It's frightening. He looks so evil.'

'But he is evil. Surely you know that?'

To Gregor it seemed everything changed when Johanne spoke. It wasn't funny anymore, but disquieting, like a bad dream.

'You must never tell anyone I said or did such a thing. Promise. I would be shot for treason,' Johanne whispered.

'Shot?'

'I believe so. Promise, Gregor, promise Mari.'

She looked from one to the other, and they gazed back, faces stricken. She scribbled over her cartoon until the paper tore and the lead of the pencil snapped.

Gregor picked up his rock again and stared into it.

'I promise.'

'Good boy.'

'I see now, I see all the creatures in the rock. I've got a fossil. Look, look Mari-Louise.'

Soon after the rat incident, the children's grandmother announced that it wasn't possible for her to stay in such an industrial area. The air raids were sure to come before long with so many factories as targets. She would be in grave danger of falling on her way down to the cellar, and if she fell it would be the end. Besides that, she had quarrelled again with Gitta, her daughter-in-law, and there was no resolution.

'I care no more for Gitta than I do for that object,' she said, gesturing to the trunk she was packing to send on to her other son in the country. 'I've been here quite long enough as it is. I must get out of this city before it's unsafe to travel and I find myself locked in.'

Their father was away, and mother confined to her room, so, on a cold winter day, Johanne and the children accompanied Grandmother to the railway. Johanne carried the old lady's travelling basket with her gloves, extra shawl, and provisions in case of delays—though she was travelling so little distance and the railways were still intact. She was attentive, for the old lady was distressed at the absence of her son to see her off, and the fact he had failed to arrange a car to take her. Johanne held her arm, bought her tickets and manoeuvred her onto the platform with the children beside her.

The trains were like huge steaming monsters, and Gregor danced with delight. It was fun to watch the goods trucks being loaded and unloaded, the tall patient horses with their warm earthy smell, and the bustle of people swept up in the rush of life. His grandmother was going away and he didn't mind. She was like a big untidy crow, always watching over him with a critical eye, fixing her gaze on Mari's birthmark and shaking her head. Mother will be happy she's going too, he thought.

'I know I won't be missed,' the grandmother said, with bitterness.

Filled with remorse, he took hold of her dry bony hand. It would be terrible to be old and to belong nowhere. He looked up at the iron girders of the station—such a dizzying height, and the pale sky beyond, and shivered with the emptiness of such a thought.

'You're cold. You didn't wear your winter coat,' the grandmother said. 'Johanne, you don't look after Gregor, he's not properly clad.' She clasped Gregor to her so his nose was buried in the stale dust of her clothes.

A piercing whistle made him jump, as a train pulled away in great clouds of steam and commotion. The steam dissolved into the cold air as a freight train rolled in to the next platform. As if emerging from the walls, a sea of policemen carrying truncheons rushed forward. The doors of the freight train were unbolted, and there, instead of cattle, the frightened faces of people stared out, blinking in the light.

'Hurry along,' a sharp voice shouted, as they were pulled and pushed into lines.

Gregor had never seen so many people, sunk into themselves, eyes downcast, shoulders hunched, their faces the colour of pale clay. They staggered on unsteady legs, arms flailing as they lost balance. He couldn't distinguish one from another.

'Hurry along.'

When they faltered, a policeman beat them into place with a truncheon. Dogs strained and barked.

'Who are they?'

'Don't let them see you staring,' the grandmother hissed. 'They're prisoners imported to work in the factories.' Her hard little eyes scanned them. 'They would be advised to get moving rather than shuffling along like ailing cattle.'

'But they look ill,' Johanne said. 'How can they work?'

'If it's a matter of eating or not eating, they'll get on with it.'

Grandmother turned her head away, and with slow, swaying gait moved towards her waiting train.

Johanne had to attend to the grandmother, help her into her seat on the train, and organise the children to stand and wave as it pulled away. When that was over, and they made back to the square, the alien people in their ragged clothes had vanished.

On the way home on the streetcar nobody spoke. Johanne's face was expressionless, frozen. It seemed to Gregor as if she'd gone, leaving a mask behind. Mari kept her head down, her hands folded in her lap.

When they reached home, their mother crept, pale and fragile, from her room to greet them.

'I'm glad the old lady has gone. The house will be lighter without her,' she muttered before drifting back upstairs.

Gregor got ready for bed and Mari and Johanne sat with him in his bedroom. Johanne was instructed to oversee their evening prayers now that grandmother had gone. Gregor knelt to say his prayer for the Fatherland. He spoke the words, as he did every night, like a mechanical toy.

Führer, my Führer, you were given to me by God. Protect and preserve my life for many years. You saved Germany in time of need. I thank you for my daily bread. Be with me. Do not leave me. Führer, my faith, my light. Hail my Führer.

He opened his eyes. Johanne's face was tight with anger. He wondered what it was he'd done wrong. He plucked at his bedspread, twisting it in his fingers.

'I refuse to listen to this again. This thing called a prayer. You can send me away. You can do what you like. I will not listen to these words.'

'But she, Grandmother, said I must always say my prayers.' Gregor closed his eyes, trying to remember exactly what she'd said. 'There are three fathers. The first is father, the second is Almighty God, and the third is Adolf Hitler. Adolf Hitler was sent by Almighty God to save our great nation.'

Johanne's hand struck him full on the cheek.

'Adolf Hitler is nobody's father.'

Mari gasped. Gregor cried out in shock and hurt. His face reddened and he buried his head on her lap.

'I'm sorry. I'm sorry,' Johanne said, her voice full of remorse. 'I never meant to hurt you. I should never have done that.'

'It doesn't matter,' Gregor whispered, blinking back his tears. He knew he must have deserved it.

'I lost my temper. You are just a little boy. One day you'll understand.'

'I want to understand now. I don't want to wait.'

'Then you must look at what's around you, and listen to what's not said.'

Gregor sat up and looked at her, trying to understand.

'Listen to what's not said? What does that mean?'

'Don't think about it now. I shouldn't say these things.' Johanne pulled him onto her lap, and kissed his head. 'I'm sorry, I'm so sorry.'

He started to sob.

'Johanne was angry about the prisoners, not with you, Gregor' Mari said. 'Come. Let's settle down now.'

He got into his bed. He wouldn't be able to sleep. When he heard them get ready to leave him, he called out for them to stay. After a long quiet time, he heard their low voices.

'Johanne, those people who came off the train—where will they go? They looked so poorly and hungry.'

'Sick or not, they'll work in munitions, making more weapons for Germany. My Papa told me. He's a foreman in the Works. They come from Poland and the east. They're forced to work from dawn until night, with no holiday, not even a Sunday, and not enough food, or anywhere to sleep.'

'What will happen to them?'

'They'll get too weak to work.'

Gregor could feel Mari's anguish in her snatched breath. He knew that she was weeping, and that Johanne and she held each other tight, even though he didn't open his eyes even a crack. He heard the relentless ticking of the clock, the rattle of a window in the chilly bathroom. He knew he was not part of the pity and terror that flowed between them, even though he felt the intensity of it. In his head he cried out and gripped the sheet between his teeth.

'Never go away,' Mari whispered. 'Never leave me, Johanne.'

The inhabitants of number 7 Gladstone Terrace were all affected by the change in Gregor. Monica was mystified. She whispered to Birdy behind the closed door of their room. What can have happened that made Gregor so distracted? She'd never known him thoughtless or forgetful before, or seen the dark rings round his eyes. He moves like the dead, she said. Hasn't he slept for days? Birdy stood at the window to observe him leave the house. She listened for his return, her face pinched with anxiety.

SA Pete was full of religious foreboding. He recognised that absent look, that way of moving, as if weightless, no longer bound by the earth. Gregor was in purgatory. He feared for his soul. He knelt on his mat, The Parson curled beside him, and prayed aloud that Gregor would resist the temptations of the Devil.

Philadelphia wandered around the house, leaning weakly against walls and furniture, telling the others how hungry she was. She had relied on Gregor for meals. She searched in the cupboards to no avail. Not enough to feed a mouse. Where did everyone keep their tins? It might become necessary to find another place to live, except that Moonlight refused to leave, and there were still days when Gregor returned laden with good things. There were times too when Ruby, irritated by them all, made plates of toast. But it wasn't the same. The way he cooked, the way he provided a meal—it had been more than food. Gregor made the place into a home, something she hadn't had since her stepfather had kicked her out.

When she wasn't at school Moonlight spent her days on the stairs, in various costumes, practising handstands, and balance-walking along the bannisters. She had a secret plan to join the circus or a travelling cabaret company. Ruby's presence made her unsettled, even angry, and she made efforts to avoid her.

Only Willoughby was unconcerned. Coming home from work he would unpack his shopping, make beans on toast and go to his room, passing the inverted Moonlight on the stairs. Whilst he ate he would listen to the sounds in the house, the whispering and scuffling of Monica, the public prayers of SA Pete, the slap of Moonlight's bare feet against the wall, her swearing when she fell. After eating he prepared his table for drawing. He forgot time. With the door open to maximise the light, the sounds of the house died away and he was lost to his work. Only when he heard Ruby singing, would he put down the charcoal, close his eyes and listen—her glorious soaring voice.

Ruby went upstairs soft-footed, stepping over the boards that creaked. She passed Moonlight, who wouldn't look at her, and went up to Willoughby's room. He was absorbed in his drawings. She stood in the doorway and willed him to turn round, but he continued to draw with silent concentration. He scarcely seemed to breathe. She went back down and changed her clothes, thinking how entertaining it would be to see how many times she had to change her dress and go upstairs before he sensed her presence. Maybe, she thought, I should undress to my underwear. She sighed. Such childish entertainment was poor distraction against the trouble of Gregor.

After the second journey downstairs and up again she was bored. People were tiresome when they concentrated so hard on their work. Wearing a sunflower-print dress, she stood in the partly closed doorway, and began to sing.

He looked round and smiled.

'At least you're glad to see me. You took ages to notice though.'

'No, I knew you were there.'

'You didn't!' She ran in and thumped him playfully in the chest. 'Can I see what you're drawing?'

He sat back to let her see the charcoal portraits.

'Who are they?'

'Nobody I know. Made them up.'

It had been like this for over a week. Once he'd stopped drawing portraits of Ruby and the other residents, the men had emerged—men with thin necks, deep-set eyes, angular shadows under the cheekbones and mouth.

'They're bizarre, these people. Frightening don't you think? Their faces are unkind. Why such ugliness? You should draw me again. Look. Me in all my glory.' She opened her arms wide. The strap of her cotton dress fell over her shoulder. 'You don't draw me anymore.'

'I will draw you again.'

'When?'

He shook his head.

'I don't know.'

Ruby wriggled round the table until she was in front of him, and placed her hands on either side of his face.

'Willo, don't become remote, like Gregor. Oh my heart is breaking.' She clutched her chest melodramatically. 'Oh, I'm so unhappy.'

The way she spoke with her slight accent, and emphasis on the word *so*, was his undoing. He put down the charcoal and wiped his hands on a rag, took her hands in his.

'Why do you always distract me, Ruby?'

'Where else can I go? Gregor has left me. He's been enchanted by Leda Godwin. I hate her. She has no idea about him, how easily he's disturbed. All she wants is her story.'

'So you come to me instead. I'm a consolation prize?'

She shrugged and widened her eyes.

'Of course. But I like you very much, and Gregor isn't my lover anyway. And you like me, don't you? I am entirely without guile.'

She always made him laugh.

'I don't know about guileless.'

'But we can lie down for a little while.'

'Would that make you happy?'

She let go of his hands and went to shut the door.

'It would cheer me up. It would make everything that's impossible seem possible again.' She put her arms round his neck. 'Yes, it would make me happy.'

'A fun way to pass the time?'

Ruby lay motionless on her back, one arm over Willoughby's chest. She'd slept briefly, then woken and started to hum quietly. Gently he extricated himself, pulled on his trousers, boiled the kettle and brought her tea. She stirred herself and leant on one elbow to drink, pulling the sheets round her. Outside it had begun to rain, warm summer rain, sudden and fierce. Willoughby sat in the chair, his hands round his cup, looking at her, she thought, as if he might draw her naked. But there was no time for that. When she'd finished her tea she sprang up and pulled on her underclothes and tights.

'Like a cat I must puff myself up, because I don't feel very strong.'

'Why do you need to be strong?' Willoughby went to her, put his arms round her waist and kissed the nape of her neck. 'You could lie down again.'

'I'm going to go to Leda Godwin and have it out with her. Will you come with me?'

Willoughby dropped his hold.

'No. You're impossible. Gregor's a free agent, Ruby. He can speak for himself.'

'He won't though. He'll go along with it all, even if it makes him kill himself.'

'Is that what you're afraid of?'

She put her hands over her face for a moment.

'Oh, I don't know. But whatever happens he'll let her unscrew all the jars of his mind, peer in for as long as she wants, and then leave them open to fester. I know the nights he can't sleep, and how little he eats. She knows nothing.'

'The jars of his mind?'

'You know what I mean. I wish you would come.'

'I won't though. I don't like the rain, and you're not his keeper. I'll be here when you get back.'

He turned back to his drawings.

The sun came out, and then the sky darkened and rain burst from the sky again. Ruby knew the place—the warehouses by the river where the actors and artists hung out. She'd heard some of them even lived there. She'd once followed Gregor, from a distance, but close enough to discover where the entrance was. Miss Godwin lived on the top floor – he'd told her that. She glanced up at the tall buildings—all those windows with criss-crossed metal bars—which windows were hers? If a fire started, how could anyone jump down from so high, or be rescued through such tiny spaces? They were artists, they hadn't thought of that. Stupid.

She was drenched; the sunflower dress clung to her skin, and her hair, plastered to her face, trickled water down her neck so she shivered. She'd forgotten a coat or umbrella. Now she had to navigate the interior of the building, corridors and stairways full of dust, old sacks and rope, and the pervasive smell of spices. She knew that smell because, when Gregor returned, it clung to his clothes.

At the top of one flight of steps she paused behind a metal pillar, and found she was in a dance studio. She hadn't expected that. It disconcerted her, seeing the dancers sprawled on the floor in their tatty rehearsal clothes, reminding her of the times she'd been taken, as a child, to watch Mama teach or rehearse. A woman in baggy trousers directed three dancers, who lifted each other on and off chairs to a steady drumbeat. It could have been her own mother. Chairs often featured in her work.

She crept past, up a narrow stairway to the top floor and opened a door. Inside a small gloomy room a woman stood with her back to the door. It's her, Ruby thought, and her heart lurched. The woman turned and fixed Ruby with a cool gaze.

'What do you want?' she asked. Ruby saw she was mistaken. It was a different face, older and darker-skinned.

'Where will I find Leda Godwin?'

'She's not in. But her space is at the end of the building, across the studio, behind the tarp. You're drenched.'

'I do know.'

'You need a coat.'

The woman went back to stacking her papers.

Ruby went on, slipped behind the tarpaulin, and saw a desk with a lamp and two chairs. There was a bookshelf made of stacked boxes, and the offending cassette recorder, but no cassette inside it. Another sheet of fabric hanging from the beams divided the space into a small kitchen with a Baby Belling stove, a table with two glasses, two mugs, and a bottle of brandy. Beyond that, there was a space, as small as a cupboard, with a mattress on the floor and more wooden box shelves for clothing. It was as if she'd set up temporary camp in the great open space of the studio, with its row of windows looking over the river.

Ruby was struck by the austerity of it all—much like Gregor's bedroom at number 7. I don't know what to do now, she thought as she turned slowly, and looked down from the window into the narrow street. The sun had emerged through dark clouds, and the wet cobbles glistened.

It struck her, looking out, that it was Leda Godwin she saw walking away from the warehouse, towards the gap between buildings that led down to the river. And it was Gregor she saw walking towards Leda. They greeted each other, Gregor with a small bow of his head, in the formal way he had. Then they disappeared round the corner.

She gripped the stone windowsill to steady herself as the blood drained from her head. How was it she had missed Leda? Had she come from another building? The deliberate way she walked, the way she greeted him, taking his hand. Terror overwhelmed Ruby, so she scarcely knew how to breathe. Was it memory or dream, that sensation deep in her gut—the end of everything dear and familiar—nonbeing, nothingness? Help me, she said. Hands to her face she shook her head, rushed out of the room, down the flights of stairs into the street.

Gregor and Leda had met by chance as Leda was leaving the warehouse. He was surprised when she took his hand and held it briefly, as if they were being introduced to each other for the first time. There was a moment of hesitation.

'Were you coming to see me?' she asked.

'I was. But maybe, after all, I prefer to be out. It doesn't matter. I wouldn't want to intrude. You're on your way somewhere.'

'I'm not really going anywhere. Just walking and thinking. You're welcome to walk with me.'

They fell into step, turned to the river and walked along the wharf side. The wind slapped the water against the wall, rippling it into dancing ribbons of silver. They looked upstream towards Tower Bridge, and then turned to walk in the other direction, as if sniffing out the sea. The rain clouds had cleared, leaving the pale blue sky streaked with thin cloud. It felt a relief to Gregor not to sit with the whirring cassette recorder, and the uncomfortable notion that strangers listened in as they sat for hours in her room.

'Leda,' he said. 'Do you mind if I call you Leda, instead of Miss Godwin?'

'Whatever you like. There's no need for formality.'

'Leda Godwin.' He smiled. If Leda wanted to walk with him that was good, friendlier than it had been before. He liked her quiet presence.

'There was a boy who lived near us,' he said, after a while. 'He came to mind last night, and I couldn't stop thinking about him. I wondered if he survived to grow up. I doubt it. He was maybe Mari's age, fourteen or so. What marked him out was that he refused to join the Hitler Youth.

'The other boys would pass by our house on a Friday night. I was too little to join, and I looked at them with longing, because I thought it would be so nice to wear the uniform and march with them. But this boy, he wouldn't join, and he looked down on them, and every week he was beaten up. Once I saw them kicking his face and dragging him through the dust, and all the time he made a terrible grunting sound. They called him a filthy pig. I saw him in the street once. He gave me this look I've never forgotten, a mixture of pity and contempt. I didn't understand why. Was it something in my face? Or did he know my father? After that I had a sense of shame, and Johanne's words only made that shame more potent. I existed between two worlds. In one my father was the great man I admired and feared. The other world could not bear too much scrutiny. It was like a lead weight in my stomach. Reality shifted shape, and nothing seemed real for long enough to make sense of the world.'

'As it has done ever since,' Leda said.

'Yes. In a way you're right.'

They turned away from the river and stopped by a patch of wasteland where a lilac bush drooped heavy scented blooms. There was a low wall to sit on. Gregor took a flask from his knapsack and poured tea. His hands moved slowly, absently, so he spilled a little. He handed Leda the cup, opened a packet of ginger biscuits and took a stack of them from the packet.

'Please eat as many as you need.' He broke one in pieces and scattered them for the birds. 'It was different for Mari Louise. She was clear, like the boy who wouldn't join Hitler Youth, and like Johanne Kuhn. God is angry with us, she said one day. The German nation is doing terrible things.

What can we do to help God? Don't you think that's remarkable, Leda, the notion of helping God? Johanne, Mari and the boy were the extraordinary ones. Everyone else I knew was under the Nazi enchantment. How my beloved sister suffered, as did Johanne. What happened to the boy? I hope he survived to grow up. He might have become a great man.'

A pigeon flew down and pecked at the biscuits. Another joined it. Gregor broke more biscuits and threw them. The birds scattered for a moment, then waddled back.

'My story becomes more painful to tell. So much of it belongs to others—as if I was flung around in other people's stories, without any direction of my own. They should be telling you, if only they could—Johanne, my father, Mari.'

'You were a child. How could it be otherwise?'

'Except once.' He put his hands to his face. 'I think there was a time—something terrible I did that changed everything. Almost unbearable. Oh but today we're meant to be resting. I'm so sorry. I'm like someone possessed.'

'It's all right.'

He turned to look at her face in profile, as if seeing her for the first time. She was enigmatic, and at the same time deeply known to him.

'Who are you? Day after day you sit so quietly listening to me, absorbing all this. What is it you want?'

She turned to look at him, her gaze detached.

'I don't ask any more than this.'

By the time Ruby remembered she was meant to modelling for the art class that evening, it was late. Willoughby would be waiting for her to come back, as she'd said she would. But that was too bad. Everything was too bad. She rushed through puddles in her haste. Her tights were drenched, and she had no coat. Two conflicting voices muttered in her head—*I couldn't bear Gregor to leave*, said one. *He won't*, said the other. *Where would he go anyway? What if Leda Godwin leaves and he goes with her? But you're used to Gregor leaving. You haven't always lived with him. But now—now it's so clear, we need each other. We are two sides of the same one thing.*

She stopped at the entrance to the art school, and shouted out loud, *shut up shut up*, before rushing through the doors and up the marble staircase. At the turn in the stairs she stopped to release a stitch and get her breath. Light poured through the stained-glass window, and she leant back against the wall. It was like being under water—green, blue, grey water moving with the current. Slowly she went on up.

They turned to look when she arrived, the circle of artists behind their easels.

'I'm so sorry I'm late.' She was still breathless.

The tutor, David Clare said, 'It doesn't matter. We've been doing exercises.' Then he came to her and asked was she all right, looking into her face with his kindly eyes.

'I got wet,' she said. 'I'm cold.'

She knew she was a good model so they forgave her unreliability.

She undressed in the side room where she kept her things, and then found she couldn't bear to be naked, not only because she was so cold. She put on a beautiful gown, silk patterned with peacock feathers, a challenge for them to draw.

On a rug in the middle of the floor, she sat with her arms clasping her bent legs. She sank her head on her knees and closed her eyes—heard the scratching of charcoal and pencil on the paper, an intake of breath, someone sniffing, the soft voice of the tutor. My mother used to draw me, she'd told Willoughby Stone.

She thought of the first time Gregor had left the house in Amsterdam. She had been a child and sick with a fever, her skin covered with red spots. It must have been measles. She imagined she was telling her story to someone like Leda—but that wouldn't do. Perhaps she would write her autobiography and everyone would want to read it. She would become immortal through her book.

When I recovered from measles, she remembered, *I went to look for Gregor in his little room, and found his bed had no blanket covering it. It was just a bare mattress with folded sheets and the pillows on top. I opened the drawers and found all his clothes gone. They said Aunt Gitta had taken him away and left nothing but a note, not even a letter, on the cabinet in the hall. Everyone in the family talked about it for days, what a terrible thing it was to take the child away. They talked all day and night. What had possessed Gitta? Gregor was happy and settled. But after all he is her son. Whatever kind of mother you think she is, he is still her son. But that didn't excuse it. The weather changed—a furious wind rattled the windows, and made the trees bend and bow, whilst inside the house was a storm of grief. If she's taken him on the ship, the crossing will be rough. He'll be so sick. I was afraid Gregor would drown in the stormy sea. I howled and ran from room to room, until Aunt Elise came and held me, sobbing and worn out.*

'What's wrong today, Ruby?' David Clare asked, when the artists had gone. 'What are you thinking about?'

She was perched on a wooden stool, hugging her knees. He drew a chair up beside her. She buried her face in his warm familiar smell of turpentine and graphite, afraid he would see her tears. He would probably think she was crying over him, so she tried to hold herself together, her body rocking slightly, her mouth opening and closing like a gasping fish. He mustn't know.

'Beautiful girl,' he said, and kissed her head. 'Beautiful darling girl.'

Soon, in a moment, she would get up and lead him into her changing room. She would let him lie beside her on the fur rug. When she was warm again, he would undress her and gaze at her body, with that look of tenderness and desire in his eyes. It was a small thing, and would make him happy.

After Ruby had parted from David Clare—he had been so apologetic that he couldn't stay with her for the evening—she went to Antonio's wearing a long red coat she'd found amongst her art room costumes, to keep warm. It would be good to eat a big plate of spaghetti, and, when he had a moment, Antonio would be sure to come to talk to her.

She sat in a dark corner and Antonio lit her candle.

'I need courage,' she told him. 'I need the restorative wine and a big plate of food. You can't imagine how hungry I am. No, Gregor is busy today and I'm alone. I am so unhappy.'

A man with a thin ponytail of dark hair played the guitar and sang quietly. Ah, how beautiful the music was, and how lovely the candlelight falling over his hands and face, turning him into gold. She gazed into space, and time passed. She didn't desire him, despite his music.

The restaurant was empty, only the staff still busy in the kitchen, a clattering of plates.

'We can never know things, can we?' she said to Antonio when he came to sit with her.

He looked puzzled, but smiled.

'We shouldn't need to examine too carefully the poor heart and all our petty struggles,' she continued. She was drunk by then. It was hard to control her voice, but everything felt fine again, even though her hands shook. She was too warm, and then cold.

'Did I ever tell you about my mother? In 1943 she was meant to be executed by the Nazis, but they let her free. It was a Dutch Nazi who saved her life. If he hadn't, I would never have been born, simple as that. I would have died inside her womb as the shot was fired and she fell. The Nazi must have been in love with her because he saved her. He begged her to speak up for him at the trials, but she wouldn't because of my poor papa. I can tell you this because I'm so drunk.' She poured another glass. 'We should be glad to be happy and simple, and thankful our lives don't make us cruel. Seize the day, don't you think, Antonio?'

'You're a beautiful woman,' he said. He gave her a handkerchief to dry her tears. 'I am very sorry you're sad, and at the same time happy for your mother that you were born. I see no cruelty in you.'

It was raining again when they left the restaurant. Ruby stopped at the bus stop and lifted her face to the sky. Under the streetlamp her wet skin glowed.

'*Singing in the rain*,' she sang softly.

'I'll get you a taxi,' Antonio said.

'No, the bus will soon come.'

He waited with her. She sang until her voice faltered and she drooped against the wall.

'Oh I can't go on. What will become of me?'

'Come home with me, Ruby.' He put his arm round her.

'You're an old man.'

'I may be old, but tonight you need looking after. I will look after you.'

Gregor lay on his back, arms folded over his chest, his eyes closed. His eyelids twitched and flickered. He longed for sleep, but his body was too wired, his heart burning with anxiety. Ruby hadn't come home. She sometimes stayed out. She would be all right. He had to trust.

On the floor, propped beside his mattress, was a photograph of Leda Godwin standing by a window, looking out onto a garden, her face half in shadow. It had been torn from a magazine and stapled to a piece of card. She held a large white cat in her arms. Beside her was a bowl of red tulips. He'd found it in one of the dance studios in the warehouse, and taken it.

Underneath the photograph was a sheet of finest quality paper, a letter to Gregor, small, even writing in blue ink, with long spaces between the words—a controlled, steady hand.

Lucifer is both the light and also the devil. Lucifer was, or is, essential to God. There can be no light without darkness. So it seems.

You asked who I am and what I do.

Through my work I want to illuminate the darkness—to bring the world of dreams to light, to recognise that nothing is quite what it seems at first to be. I try to see you clearly and to listen with attention. I'm trying to capture, through theatre, an impression, moments when the truth, half-known, can be sensed, though not understood through logic and language. Sometimes we see more clearly with the heart. But that doesn't really tell you anything, does it?

My work is the expression of dreams, of events, of stories half-remembered. I strive to be truthful, to you, to everything you tell me. How do I know when I am truthful? Maybe it's easier to recognise when I'm not. There is no compromise, but I know no other way. I ask everything of you, and at the same time nothing—as you must of me.

Willoughby sat in his room at the top of the house, face and hands smeared with charcoal dust. The landing outside his open door was suffused in greenish light, the leaves rustled and tapped against the long window. He heard the beat of pigeons' wings in the tree, and Moonlight shouting at her mother downstairs.

He drew quietly until it was too dark to see, faces on sheets of paper he pinned to the wall. The portraits were not Gregor, but a man, maybe a little like him in feature, and quite as convincing as if he'd drawn from life.

He stood back to look. It was a hard handsome face—a man of some standing—intelligent, determined, sure of his place in the world. Sometimes this unknown face disturbed him. He had the odd notion that he'd seen it somewhere, a sense of déjà vu. He would go to the window then, and stare out into the distance, over the rooftops and chimneys, until he gained equilibrium.

He listened for Ruby, he spoke her name, but she didn't come. She'd said she was coming back that night. He supposed, being Ruby, she had found a more exciting alternative. He didn't draw her any longer. It was best not. She already filled his mind too much.

'Your cousin came here yesterday,' Leda said. 'We didn't meet. She'd gone when I got back.'

She stood with her back to the window, her face in shadow.

'I didn't know. She didn't come home last night.'

'Why should you know? My colleague downstairs found her. She came in, soaking wet from the rain, asking to see me. I could smell her perfume. That's how I knew who it was. Nothing else, no message, nothing disturbed, though I imagine she had a good look around.'

Gregor picked up one of the pebbles that lay on her table, warmed it in his hand.

'Ruby can't bear too much sadness,' he said quietly. 'She wants me to be happy and will do anything to protect me.' He sat down, the pebble resting in the palm of his hand. 'It was always this way, even when she was very little. There was enough sadness around—too much for a girl with such a sunny temperament to bear.'

He looked at the flecks of silver in the pebble. Funny that Leda collected them too, as he had done as a child.

'The family in Amsterdam, they all asked too much of Ruby.' He fell silent, absently rubbing the tip of his finger over the ridges and hollows.

There had been an afternoon, long ago, when they were both children. The whole family had gathered in the drawing room in Amsterdam—Aunt Hedda and the grandparents, Aunt Marianne and Aunt Elise. It was autumn, wild wind and rain. Inside, the teapot had been set to warm on the tea-lights. Aunt Marianne had made ginger biscuits. Ruby sat on a rug on the floor sucking a biscuit to make it soft. That was the afternoon when Hedda told them about the spider. She had never told them about her weeks in prison before. It was something nobody mentioned.

'Where are you?' Leda asked. 'You seem so far away.'

'I was thinking of Ruby's mother, Hedda, and the grief there was in that house in the woods—how they looked to Ruby to bring the only joy. As if she was a little automaton, a pretty doll, endlessly resourceful. They called her Dora— the adored child. They loved her, of course, but it must have been a strain. No wonder she can't bear too much sadness.'

'She had you.'

'No, I wasn't always there. After two years of peace, my mother took me away. Over the years we often came back and left again. She'd fall out with the family and off we'd go again, from country to country in search of my father. Awful.

'But I want to tell you about Ruby's mother, Hedda— that afternoon has just come to me so clearly.'

Leda took the cassette recorder from the shelf and put it on the desk.

'You can start recording when you're ready.'

Leda pressed the *record* button. She went back to stand by the window, turned away from Gregor, as if she could listen better if she gazed out over the river.

I loved my mother's older sister Hedda. I always wished I'd known her before the rise of Hitler, when she was young, those years when she had her dance school in Amsterdam and was such a beautiful dancer. She was changed after the Gestapo arrested her and Ruby's father—silent, as if in some way she was still locked away in that cell waiting for her execution. Then, from time to time, something would touch her—maybe Aunt Elise playing the piano, or a visit from one of her old pupils, and it would be as if she woke from a trance—her amazing, vivid spirit would shine. I would catch a glimpse of what she had once been.

That autumn—the family sitting by the fire, Ruby on the rug chewing her biscuit, the curtains shutting out the wild night— Hedda told us, for the first time, about prison. We almost held our breath as we listened, for fear the story might end before it began.

The spider was the size of my thumbnail, she said. The spider, my spider, spun a web in the corner of the cell, so light from the tiny window caught her threads. When the sun shone, they would shimmer, and I would imagine the blue sky outside. My spider was the only other living creature with me in that cell. I believed she knew all my thoughts, and that I understood her in return. It was a wonderful thing we shared.

One morning I saw a fly had found a way in. There we were— the three of us trapped together. The spider waited motionless until the careless creature flew too close to the web, then she darted out, quicker than I'd ever seen anything move. There was a brief and frantic buzzing, and it was over. The fly paralysed, dead. I felt the spider's triumph, but at the same time the fly's desperation—as if I inhabited both creatures at once. I froze, and it took a great effort to break out and move. I was gasping for breath, terrified. When the Gestapo come to take me to my execution, I thought, I will shout and dance all my terror and rage, noisy and wild as the fly. I will not go in silence.

After Hedda's story nobody spoke. I was scared. I didn't know what to do. Ruby knew. She climbed onto the table, her little feet finding a place amongst the teacups, and danced as she sang about a wooden doll. Ruby. She bowed and waited for the applause, and Hedda's story was pushed aside. That's what she's like. That's what she's still doing when she talks on and on. Do you understand now, Leda?

Ruby returned home the next morning. The rain was over and the day cool and cloudy. She filled the bath, poured in lavender bath oil, undressed and slipped into the water. Antonio had been kind. She had slept in a long white cotton nightgown, like a virgin. He had knelt and prayed in the corner of the room. She thought he'd whispered the rosary in Italian. *Ave O Maria, piena di grazia*...how beautiful it was. She had floated away, at peace. Sometime in the night he had lain beside her, a candle burning to keep away evil. It had been sweet and good, the room had spun, and she'd felt his dry hand on her forehead.

Oh Lord, did I really sleep with three men yesterday, she thought? Maybe not with Antonio—after all, he's an old man. Ah, but I think I most likely did. I am no virgin. It probably made us all feel better, as long as the men don't know about each other.

She giggled and slipped down the bath so the water lapped around her ears, then emerged and gazed up at the patches on the ceiling where the paint had peeled away. She'd drifted asleep in the warmth of Antonio's bed, woke wondering where she was, and had gone straight to sleep again. Ah, sleep was so good.

The water was lukewarm, so she turned on the hot tap. The bathroom steamed up. She wanted to let go, emerge forever from the weight of Gregor's misery and guilt. It was as hard to live with as her mother's anger and grief had been. She blew bubbles in the water, surfaced, laughing, and sang a few scales, listening to her voice echoing round the room. I can be whatever I want. We will be happy, be glad for everything. I won't allow Leda Godwin to drag Gregor down.

She paused in her singing and heard someone on the stairs. She called out. Gregor answered.

'Gregor, the ghost of the night, you're back at last.'

He stood at the half open door.

'It's you who are back Ruby. We didn't know where you'd gone, away all night. Willoughby was worried too.'

'You know I'm all right. I can look after myself. Why do you always come peering at me, as if I'm a sick child? Especially as you're the one who's always disappearing, whilst I'm positively stranded in the house waiting to see when you'll return.'

'I returned. Last night. The electricity went down and Willoughby fixed it.'

'So a romantic night of candles. How glad I am to have missed it. No more drawing for Willoughby, no food for the Lame Ducks. A joyful waste of time by candlelight.'

Gregor sat on the floor and leant back against the wall.

'By torchlight I made them bread and jam, and a salad. They were very happy.'

In answer, she filled the sponge with water and squeezed it over her hair.

'Do you remember that time when we were little, just after Uncle Ben came back, when we had a funeral for the dead rabbit?' he said.

'No. I don't remember. We were always having funerals for dead animals.'

'I think you do. I was thinking about Uncle Ben last night,' he continued. 'How thin he was when he came back, like a skeleton. He sat with Aunt Hedda, they needed each other so badly, but they couldn't talk about what had happened, even to each other. I was old enough to understand that. I remember we found a dead rabbit in the forest. You wanted to punish the person who'd shot it, and Uncle Ben helped us plan a funeral. That's when I saw the number on his arm for the first and only time.'

'Shut up, shut up.'

He was shocked into silence by her ferocity.

Ruby sank her head under the water, and then stood up so quickly the water splashed onto Gregor. 'Hand me that towel.'

Gregor wrapped the towel round her, and she padded out of the bathroom leaving a trail of water behind her.

'I think you and Leda Godwin should make a comedy about Adolf Hitler and the Third Reich—a really funny play would be marvellous. We could have Eva Braun and the golden haired Mädchen as bunny girls, and I'd be delighted to star in it with a bag over my head.'

'We must be brave, Ruby,' he said, so quietly he didn't think she'd heard.

'Brave for what?' she shouted from the landing. 'I have never in my life been brave. I leave that to everyone else, especially you.'

Ruby dressed and went down to the kitchen to heat a tin of noodle soup. SA Pete had come in and made tea, and stood, holding his mug and leaning against the wall, watching her, hoping to be companionable. She sloshed soup over the gas ring, and slammed the bowls down on the table.

'Don't tell me to pray. It doesn't work. I tried it.'

He hunched into his leather jacket.

'I don't know how to help you. I'm at a loss.'

'It's not me who needs help, is it? You see how it is. Everyone in the house sees. I don't know if Gregor slept last night, because I wasn't here, but I know he hasn't slept all the other nights. He walks up and down the landing like a weird ghost. Then he shuts himself in his room and mutters away.' She took out a loaf of bread and cut hunks off it. 'Sit down, let's eat soup, for want of anything more useful to do.'

He sat down, took a piece of bread.

Ruby laughed.

'I've just thought, I suppose, before you saw the light, you could have sorted her out.'

He looked up at her, bewildered.

'Yes, you and your old pals. You could have dispatched Leda Godwin. You know what to do after all.' She laughed again and raised her arms. 'Oh Lord, lead me not into temptation, deliver me from evil.'

'I care about you, Ruby,' he said.

'Oh.' She saw tears in his eyes. 'I don't know why. I'm a pretty awful person really.' Then her own eyes filled with tears. She blinked, looked down, stirred the soup, and let it drip from the spoon.

'What I'd like is someone to busk with. It's so lonely on my own, just me and the terrifying public.' She smiled her brilliant smile at him. 'You can't play anything can you? Or sing?'

'Only hymns.'

'That's not really what I had in mind. But you could come with me—you and the dog. You don't have to do anything more than wear a stylish hat, and look as if you're part of my little show. We'll get more money if The Parson comes. Maybe Moonlight would come too. You know what they say about animals and children.'

There was a change in my sister. Something terrible must have caused this change—but I didn't know what or why.

Mari and Johanne no longer included me, unless they had to. There were secrets. One afternoon I was tired of playing on my own. I went to look for my sister, but her bedroom was empty. My mother's door was locked. I rattled the doorknob, but if she was there, she was either asleep or chose not to answer. I stood alone in the hall and heard the great wall clock ticking in the silence. It felt odd, frightening, as if I was the only person left in the house—where were Johanne, and the two servants that day? Where was everyone? There was nothing I could think of to do but to go down to father's forbidden study.

It was there I found Mari sitting on the chair by the door, staring out of the window at the rain. I startled her, and she looked guilty, as if I'd discovered her doing something wrong. She told me to go away, but I refused. I asked why she was there and reminded her that we weren't allowed to disturb father. That doesn't matter now, she told me. I have to try. What do you have to try, I asked? But she refused to tell me anything. You have to try, I repeated. Try everything, even though you don't know what everything is. I hoped she would be persuaded to explain, but I must only have irritated her. I pressed my ear to the door and heard Father's voice, a low drone, then sharp, as if he was angry. He's on the telephone, I said. I know that, Mari said. She was waiting until he'd ended his call before knocking on the door.

But when Father's voice rose to a shout and the receiver slammed down, she didn't move. She slid off the chair to sit on the floor, her back to the wall and head on her knees. *Tomorrow I'll go*, she said. *Today is the wrong day. He won't listen today because he's too angry. I know that. Tomorrow I'll go. I'll go with you. We can be strong together*, I pleaded. *I am very strong now. Not strong enough*, she replied, sadly.

The following day, when I asked if she'd spoken to him, she refused to discuss it. *It's hopeless*, she said.

I knew I was more of a burden to her than a comfort.

I played alone with my chessboard and pieces. Sometimes the King and Queen were Father and Mother, and I would create fights between them. I would swoop down, the Omnipresent God, and protect my mother with the knights and an army of pawns. Sometimes the Black King was Adolf Hitler fighting the allies. I made up my own stories, moved my characters and whispered their lines. I made a world where Angelia came back. She was the White Queen and I was her King, and we created our own castle, attended with gardeners and servants.

I often walked round the house, following different routes—there were many corridors and staircases. My sister and Johanne had secrets. I played quietly so I could listen to what they were talking about, whilst pretending to be busy. I followed them with silent steps and hid behind corners. Once I even got into a cupboard. I heard something about a baby with only a number for a name. Once I found a pile of little clothes folded in a suitcase on Mari's bed. I unfolded them. They smelt of old things, of dust and damp. I tried to fold the clothes as I'd found them, afraid I'd be discovered, like Bluebeard's wife—you know the story, Leda?

There was a change in Mari. One day something happened and after that she never laughed again. The change was sudden and seemed final. We'd been happy, and then, like a blow to my heart, that time was over.

Why can't I remember what it was, Leda? I want to remember.

The spools of the cassette whirred. Light and shade moved over the walls as the clouds obscured the sun. After a while, as Gregor hadn't spoken, Leda switched the *record* button off.

Gregor sighed.

'I'm sorry.'

'There's nothing to apologise for.'

'I need to go now.' He stood up, pushed the chair back under the desk and reached for his coat.

'It will come back to you, if you need it enough, Gregor. But do you want to remember? You look so sad.'

He glanced at her, lowered his eyes again.

'I'm talking of the event that changed everything for your sister. I'm certain it will come back to you, in time, if you need to know.'

'I do need to know.' He nodded. 'I'm sure of that.'

As he moved to leave, she said something softly, so he might not have heard—except that she so rarely spoke about herself and, as he never liked to ask anything, he was attuned to listen. He thought he heard her say that she trained her mind by manipulating her dreams.

'Your dreams?'

He turned back to her.

'I've taught myself to fly in my dreams.'

'How is that training your mind?'

She hesitated. He thought she wouldn't answer, and regretted asking.

'Now I can fly, I'll work on moving things round the room, and then beyond.'

'Really move?'

'Yes. Really. So when I wake they'll be in a different place.' She smiled. 'I will have to remember, when I wake up, where I moved them to.'

He smiled too. He thought about Ruby. He could imagine her saying isn't it hard enough to find things when you're awake, without throwing them round in your sleep?

'Everything you need to remember will come back to you. I know that.'

Spring afternoon 1943, Essen

Gregor loved it when Johanne and Mari took him on the streetcar down into the city. He knelt up tall on the seat to see through the window. They crossed a millstream, the water bubbling, iron-grey. Rattling along by the factories, everything seemed so different from their house on the hill,

'No fish there,' Johanne said. 'Swum away somewhere they can breathe.'

Breathe? Did fish breathe?

A shadow crossed the sun as the streetcar passed through the soot-covered foundries with their high walls, and the wind caught a fragment of red cloth flapping it against two great metal gates.

When they climbed down from the streetcar, there was that leaden, sulphurous smell. Sometimes it wafted up to their house, but here it made his nostrils sting. Gregor brushed his hand along the wall to see how thick the dirt was, and sniffed his fingers. Coal dust. He rubbed it out on his coat sleeve.

They were going to visit Johanne's parents, who lived in one of the workers' cottages. They reached the wall of the cemetery and took a shortcut that went by the headstones and the old linden trees, and through the opposite gate by an old chapel and an empty school. It started to rain suddenly and fiercely, so they stopped to take shelter in an open shed where buckets, plant pots and vases were stacked amidst broken gravestones.

They huddled and stared at the dripping trees and the empty school.

'It's so different,' Johanne said. 'What is it used for now?'

A dense barrier of barbed wire, looped round and along the top of the schoolyard wall, ensured there was no way in or out, except through tall iron gates with spikes on the top. The windows were boarded up with slats of wood, so little light could penetrate.

As they sheltered, they heard the sound of dogs barking, and the harsh voice of commands. Gregor stepped closer to Johanne and grabbed her hand. The rain on the tin roof of the shed had been loud so they hadn't heard them coming, but now they saw the crocodile of girls led by guards, stumbling along the path between the gravestones, towards the iron gates. Their heads were shaved close, scored with cuts and scabs. As they came closer Gregor saw their bowed and bony legs, their feet wound in filthy rags. They moved like old women, eyes cast down.

There was one little girl whimpering, mouth gaping with misery, as a guard flicked a whip over her head. He struck her over and over, laughing as she cowered behind the others.

'Are you scared?' he taunted.

Her whole body shook with terror. She tried to cover her head.

'Leave her alone,' Johanne shouted, striding out from their shelter to face him. 'You evil bully.'

The man with the whip stopped. Gregor saw something change in his expression, a kind of embarrassment, as if he'd been caught out. He shrugged and laughed once more, as the great iron gates opened and the girls staggered through. As the last girl disappeared into the darkness of the school hall, the doors were shut and locked behind them.

Gregor turned to his sister, but she didn't see him. Her mouth opened and closed, as if she gasped for air.

Gregor knew it was up to him. Mari had changed and something was terribly wrong—as if she'd broken inside. He couldn't tell his mother. She was too lost in her own troubles. It was possible his father might listen.

One night, soon after they'd seen the girls, he waited outside the door of his father's study. He tried to think what to say when his father found him. He prayed he would know—that the words would come. *Dear God, help me explain. Dear God…* He held his breath and counted to fifty. Fifty might be a lucky number.

Ernst von Loeben emerged from his study.

'What are you doing skulking outside my room?'

'I'm thinking,' Gregor replied.

Ernst stood back to appraise him.

'You look fragile, puny even, as if you've outgrown your strength.'

Gregor blinked, looked directly into his father's eyes.

'Don't look at me in that way.'

Gregor looked down at his feet.

'Come in, my boy. I too am alone. You can think in my room. We can think together, ha. When I've finished we will go out for a drive to the Villa.'

Gregor scrambled down from the chair and followed his father into the forbidden study.

'Yes. Sit down. Busy yourself while I work. You like drawing and writing?'

'Yes Father.'

'Here you are then, paper and pens. Draw and write as you like.'

Gregor sat opposite Ernst at the big oak desk. He thought for a moment, gazing at the beautiful silver-topped glass inkwells, and the pens with their golden nibs. He reached for one, nervously, as if it might sting him, and dipped it into the ink. Immediately he made a blot on the paper. He scratched lines outwards from the blot to make a spider's web. He could hear Ernst breathe and sigh. He glanced up and saw a patch of pink baldness at the top of his head.

After a while, Ernst got up. He paced from door to window to cabinet, where he poured whisky into a tumbler, filled it with soda, and drank deeply. He poured more, drank, and paced to the desk and around it once. Gregor watched him furtively as he stopped in front of the wall mirror. He put his tumbler down, took a comb from his pocket and ran it through his thick wave of hair.

'Do you think I'm a handsome man?' he asked Gregor.

'Yes, Father.'

'I think so too. Your mother, like me, is blessed with a kind of beauty. It's unfortunate your sister turned out stained.' He sighed. 'It's a scourge on the family.'

'I don't think that,' Gregor said timidly.

Ernst igored him.

'Your mother should be caring for you properly. Her continual absence piques me. Her role is to be a wife and a mother, and she reneges continually, sick or deranged, or both, and it makes me mad. It's a great strain for me.' He sat down heavily beside Gregor, and pushed the spider drawing away. His breath smelt of alcohol and cigars—the smell of important men. A muscle in his left cheek twitched. 'I'm talking to you, man to man. I tell you, your mother has no idea. I feel I'm walking on ice, everything about to collapse under and around me, and worse because of her father's history.' His eyes seemed to protrude as he looked at Gregor. 'Do you understand?'

'I don't know, Father.'

'Your grandfather was a traitor to the Nazi Party. Association with him is likely to blight me too. I cling to favour like a drowning man to a raft. If I fall we lose everything, home, status, wealth, power. I'd have no way to justify myself. They won't listen. Do you understand now?'

Gregor nodded, unable to utter a word.

Ernst opened a drawer in his desk and took out a photograph. He passed it to Gregor.

'Do you know who she is?'

Gregor gazed at the photograph. Angelia smiled out at him, her hand at her throat, her hair falling in curls over her shoulders. He blushed, felt his heart quicken.

'I loved her,' Ernst said. 'She was a beautiful woman.'

'I love her too, Father,' Gregor whispered. His mouth felt dry as dust.

'She is gone. Gone forever.' Tears swam into Ernst's eyes. 'Nothing has been right since the day I let her go.'

Had she died, where had she gone? Angelia. The questions rose into Gregor's throat, and froze before he could voice them. It was hopeless.

'Are you strong, son?'

'Yes.'

'Fight me then.'

'I'm not that strong.'

'Try.'

Gregor stood up nervously. He wanted to say, you are bigger than me, but dared not. Ernst took off his jacket and rolled up his shirtsleeves, and Gregor did the same. They stood away from the desk and faced each other. As Ernst parried, Gregor sprang towards him and clutched his thick wrists, but Ernst twisted from his grip, and in one movement of his arm felled his son. He turned Gregor onto his back and sat astride him. He laughed.

'I can't Daddy. I'm sorry, I'm not very strong yet.'

'Indeed. We'll have to practise. Stand up.'

Again he waited for Gregor's feeble assault, and again he struck him to the floor.

'No more, please.' Gregor's chest hurt.

'Don't you understand. I'm helping you. It's necessary you learn to defend yourself. Is that clear?'

Gregor looked up from the floor at Ernst's face, the black holes of his nostrils, the thin dark line of his mouth. The weight of his father's body pressing into his stomach and ribs made it hard to speak.

'Are you feeble, like a girl?' Ernst got to his feet and stood over Gregor, one foot pressed on his stomach. 'Women have no strength. They have to rely on us men. Get up now.' He prodded him up.

Gregor stood slowly, refusing to respond to his father's booted foot. There was something inside him now that felt like strength—defiance, a burning resentment.

'We're all prisoners,' he said quietly.

'What are you saying?'

'I've seen them, they're just girls but they're made to work like men. But I'm a prisoner too.'

'Who? What?'

'I was with Joanne and Mari-Louise, and we saw them, locked up behind barbed wire. Just girls, no bigger than me.'

His father's face turned cold and disinterested. He shrugged.

'They are prisoners of war, the Poles, the Ukrainians, inferiors. The work they do is necessary for our country. If they're driven hard it's because they're lazy. Sometimes cruelty is necessary for the greater good.' He paused, smiled. 'For the greater good,' he raised his voice. 'Say it after me.'

Gregor shook his head.

'You won't.' He laughed abruptly. 'Oh well. Tiresome it is at times, I agree. The greater good! Sit down again. Get on with your drawing.'

Ernst went to the mirror again, peered at his face, picked at a scab on his chin, put the dried blood in his mouth and swallowed.

'Hitler is not a handsome man. Der Führer.' He looked through the mirror at the portrait over his desk. 'Nondescript, pasty-faced, weak about the jowls. None of them are much as specimens. Göring is like a toad. What do you think, Gregor? An ugly old toad.'

Gregor concentrated on drawing a chessboard, blanking in the squares with dark ink. He didn't dare to look up. Was it possible his father didn't care for Hitler after all?

'Well, don't you agree?'

'Yes Father.' Warming to the idea, he said, 'Der Führer is like a rat. Johanne drew him once.'

'Drew him?'

'With a tail and rat teeth. It was funny.'

'Where did she draw him?'

'On a piece of paper, one day when it rained and we couldn't go out.'

Gregor's voice faded away. It seemed as if a dark red shadow had come over Ernst's face. He collapsed on the chair at his desk and put his head in his hands.

'Do you have the drawing still?'

'No. We burnt it in the fire.'

'Do you know what you've said? No. No, you don't. I will have to send you away to think about it.' He flapped his hand as if shoeing flies. 'Off you go. Scarper.'

'But you said we would drive to the Villa.'

'I've changed my mind,' he raised his voice, suddenly fierce. 'I'm tired. Go away and pray for deliverance and all that. I'm sick of you all. I'm sick of the world.'

In London, Gregor lay in bed listening to the incessant drip of water falling from the leaky guttering, the coming and going of cars down in the street. I will fly in my dream, he thought. He sank into sleep and found he was floating. A little later, when he woke, he distinctly remembered the sensation of leaving the ground. I know how to fly, he said, with a sense of amazement. I remember the great effort—a kicking action of both legs, like swimming butterfly stroke. He remembered how he'd often dreamed of flying as a child, flying high enough to touch the corners of a room, and to hover, like a dragonfly with iridescent wings, over people's heads.

He sat up in bed and thought about Leda Godwin. What did she look like, her pale face asleep on the pillow? He imagined her dreaming—holding swan's down on the palm of her hand, blowing gently so it fluttered to the ground.

She was often in his mind now. He spoke her name, imagined telling her things, and he was ashamed, for it felt like being a child again and loving Angelia. The smell of shame made him nauseous.

Can you smell things in dreams, he wondered?

He slept and dreamed again, but this time not of flying, or of moving feathers around his room. He was a little child, dressed in lederhosen and braces embroidered with Edelweiss, the swastika sewn on his sleeve. He was in a café with his father and other important gentlemen in their uniforms. In the corner of the café was a table of cakes, and he could smell the warm sugary aroma of vanilla and strawberry. With strong hands tight round Gregor's waist, his father lifted him onto a table. Someone played the piano, and Gregor danced, lifting his knees high and waving his arms. He loved the feeling of moving with the music. The men clapped in time to his dance.

But as soon as he rejoiced, everything turned. He had to be punished for dancing on the table in his shoes. And then it was another child, another little boy, dancing, whilst Gregor watched, his hands pinned to his sides so he couldn't move. The men drank and smoked and jeered.

You have laid it all to waste, his father said—his voice cold and clipped. *You're not worthy. And because of that you'll be dunked in the latrines. That is the punishment for everyone who lays it all to waste.*

His father and der Führer, one on either side of him, marched Gregor towards the latrines. *Do you understand,* der Führer said, *it is essential to understand? If we don't understand, everything will be repeated over and over again, the same old errors. After the dunking you will see clearly.* Der Führer's mouth worked—the rat teeth, the little moustache that looked like a rodent's lip. *You will see clearly. You must be punished because there's no other way.* They held him high by his ankles, dangling him over the black swirling shit.

He woke and shot up in bed, fighting for his breath.

'It was real,' he shouted. 'It was real.'

He collapsed back on the mattress, afraid to sleep again. But sleep kept pulling at him, his limbs heavy, as if drugged, pulling him down into the latrine. The shit, the stench of it in his nose and mouth as the Two Fathers lifted and dropped him by his legs, and he kept forcing himself awake. He sobbed and writhed.

'I'm drowning. Help me, help me, I can't see you.'

Light filled the room. He felt a hand on his chest. He breathed again.

Gregor's cries, shocking in their terror, woke Willoughby. Without hesitation he staggered out of bed, pulled on his trousers and stumbled across to Gregor's room. There, in a shaft of blue moonlight, he saw Gregor writhing in a mess of blankets. He said his name, switched on the lamp and crouched beside him. Gregor's eyes opened. He stared for a moment, like a mad man.

'Oh, my friend, I'm glad you came.' His voice was a dry whisper. 'I had the most terrible dreams—a river of shit and blood, so rank I breathed in the stench.'

'I heard you calling.'

'I'm sorry.'

'It doesn't matter. I sleep very lightly. I'll bring us tea. If you don't mind me leaving you while I brew?'

'Not at all. It's over. I remember now. I know what happened.'

Willoughby made tea and returned to Gregor. He put the mug next to his mattress. He was unsure if Gregor was asleep again. The light of dawn had blanched the moon. The birds sang. Then he saw his face, wet with tears. He stepped backwards, not wanting to intrude. But Gregor didn't appear to have seen him anyway.

He left the room, shut the door quietly and stood on the landing, listening a moment. There was something in Gregor's face—sorrow, the bewildered child—but he'd seen that before. It was something else—something ageless, impersonal, detached. He couldn't put this new thing into words. It shimmered, like a white mist that would dissipate if he didn't give it form. His fingers ached to pick up the charcoal and draw.

They came to me after I woke from a hideous dream, Leda. The truth came, as you said it would. Willoughby Stone burst into my room. I must have called out, and he came, put his hand on my chest. He went to make tea. As he left the room, in that moment, I remembered. The slave workers, the girls from the East. It was after we saw them, going into their barracks in an old chapel, that Mari changed. She was too frail to bear the weight of pity, of horror. I see now, I understand.

The terrible thing is they looked hideous to me. I stared at the prisoner girls. I couldn't help it because I'd never seen anything like them. They were terrifying. To me they seemed scarcely human. They smelt of farm animals. I can't talk...

Gregor turned off the tape recorder. He and Leda looked at each other across the table. They held each other's gaze for seconds.

'You don't judge me?' he said at last.

She shook her head, without taking her eyes from him.

'Who am I to do that?'

He looked away. Her focus was too much. Outside, someone called goodbye; on the floor below, an accompanist beat a drum for dance class.

'I was repelled and frightened,' Gregor said. 'But it wasn't only that. It was worse. I hated those poor slave workers because they changed my sister. I saw what they did to her.'

'And what did the good citizens of Essen do? I think I can answer that,' Leda said quietly. 'They ignored them. They ignored all the prisoners who were treated as slaves. There were other troubles after all—the prisoners were just one more horror that that they could do nothing about. As time went on people would no longer notice those pitiful girls trailing down narrow streets. Would they? And if they did, what could they do? They'd take another route home to avoid hearing the screams. The prisoners were, after all, mostly Jews, Poles and other inferiors. People could have done something, but they didn't. You were a child, Gregor. You were trying to grow. What could you, or your sister, do?'

But Mari-Louise tried to do something. She tried.

It was only a few weeks later. By then everything had changed. I was on the streetcar again, with Mari and Johanne, but the bombs had fallen by then. I saw streets of ruined houses, crowds of people shuffling by with their carts and bundles—so long ago it's like watching myself in a film—inconsequential, but I remember, under the seat opposite me, a crust of dirty bread, and a bee crawling along the window rim. I thought how good it would be to give bread and honey to the poor people whose houses had been bombed.

I see myself, jumping down from the streetcar, face white as a ghost, running after Johanne and Mari, trying to keep up, bewildered and fretful. They said we were going on a picnic to the woods. We will come later for you, they said, but first you must wait with Johanne's mother.

We arrived at Johanne's house, a dark room with a sweet acrid smell of smoke. I remember a tiny old lady, folding sheets. Mari and Johanne helped her, folding wet sheets and clothes and draping them round the fire.

Johanne showed me how to make stitches on white cotton with blue thread and a big needle. I didn't understand why I should, but I did as she asked, sensing the tension and urgency. I pretended to stitch as I listened to them, whispering about a prisoner of war and her baby boy. Not the enemy, the old lady hissed—the Poles are not the enemy. Hitler is the enemy. I sat rigid, straining to hear. Sometimes they stopped and looked at me, and I pretended to be intent on my sewing.

Johanne packed a basket with a bottle of milk and the tiny clothes they'd been making, and she and Mari made to leave me with Johanne's mother. I jumped from my stool and clung to Mari's sleeve, but she disentangled my fingers. Later we will come, Mari said. Wait here. You must be good and stop crying. We'll be back very soon.

Johanne's mother made me sit beside her by the steaming sheets and the fire. Her ugly face changed when she talked about Mari. Her eyes grew silky. Your sister is a good girl, she said. There are many bad people now, folk turned rotten to the core. But Mari-Louise is a beautiful girl. If you grow up like her you'll be a good person too. Will you try? She smiled at me and stroked my hair, and for a moment I had a feeling of great warmth, of love.

But I wanted to go to the toilet and I was too shy to ask. My gut ached with holding on, and in the end I wet my trousers. They said it didn't matter, but I was full of shame when Mari and Johanne returned. I felt the humiliation like a stain over everything that had felt good.

I'm trying to grasp something now, Leda, just as I was then.

On my birthday my father gave me a portrait of a soldier in uniform. I would look at the face of this soldier boy on my wall, and list all the virtues I must try to attain. Strength, courage, bravery, endurance—but the more I gazed at his clear, cold face, the more fearful, timid and confused I felt. I was failing, despite my prayers, despite my hours of exercise with the rocks in the garden. I was as far as I could be from the young brave soldier on my bedroom wall. I was lost. I am lost.

Ruby stood in the doorway of Gregor's room.

'What are you doing on the floor?'

He was sitting with his back to the wall, head bent over a pad of paper that rested on his knees.

'I'm writing.'

'To Leda Godwin?'

He covered the page with his hand.

'It's all right. I'm not going to snatch it away.'

'I'm writing a letter to my sister.'

'Mari-Louise. But she's not alive.'

He looked up. She saw his eyes dark-ringed with exhaustion.

'She's dead,' Ruby continued. 'I'm sure that's true isn't it? Where else could she be?'

'It's not that kind of letter.'

Sun streamed through the window lighting up his face. She knelt beside him, put her hands over his to stop him writing and, briefly, rested her forehead on her hands, so her hair streamed over the letter. She sat up again, looked him in the eyes.

'Gregor we haven't busked. Not for weeks. It's the most beautiful day. Everyone will be out. We could make a lot of money, and go for dinner afterwards, like we used to. Please.'

'I can't. Not now.'

'When?'

'I haven't the heart for it.'

She sighed and got to her feet.

'It's like living in a mental asylum. The only sane person in the house is Willoughby Stone, and I wonder about him sometimes.' She tiptoed to the door with exaggerated care. 'We'll be in mourning soon. You can blaze the trail of grief. What am I going to do? Oh, poor me.'

Philadelphia was sitting on the stairs, smoking a cigarette, a mug of cold tea beside her.

'I'm so unhappy,' Ruby said, stepping round her.

'So am I.'

'You're always unhappy. I think you should allow me that indulgence for a change. Give me a drag of that.' Philadelphia handed the cigarette to her, and she sucked in the smoke as if her survival depended on it. She brushed the ash off her dress. 'He sits there all day like a ghost and refuses to come out busking, or to go anywhere. Except wherever it is he goes alone. Soon there'll be no money, except what I get from modelling. I miss the street, the crowds, and the way, sometimes, someone stops in the middle of all the rush, and then it's as if I play just for them.

I can do it because Gregor is there beside me. Now, without him, I'm nothing.' She paused, waiting for Philadelphia's response.

'I asked SA Pete,' she continued. 'He said he'd come with me, but he can't do an act. Imagine. He'd be calling out to God, and everyone would scuttle past, heads down.'

'Moonlight will go with you.'

'Moonlight? What a bizarre idea.'

Philadelphia drew on her cigarette and blew the smoke from her mouth.

'She likes prancing about in costume.'

'Maybe we should all go. Phil, you can come too.'

'Me? I can't play or sing or anything.'

'I'll buy you dinner afterwards. Just come and watch, and try to look impressed. It's desperate being alone.'

Birdy and Monica were in the kitchen. Birdy stood by the table watching Monica weighing eggs. The kitchen table was covered with a mess of broken shells and egg white. Egg yoke was spattered over the walls, and everything smelt of rum.

'Christ, it looks worse than ever in here.' Ruby looked around in amazement. 'It's never been the same since Gregor gave up cooking. What the hell are you doing?'

'Making eggnog,' Monica said, and her head wobbled. 'We have colds.'

'Ah, of course, the obvious remedy. I want you to come busking. Fresh air will do you good. Pretend to look interested in me, all those things. Can you manage that?'

Birdy clasped her hands together and looked from one to the other, her eyes bright. Monica said nothing.

'Fine, that's settled then.' Ruby paused at the kitchen door. 'Why weigh the eggs?'

'To find out if they're large, medium or small.'

'Why?'

'Because it's important.'

Ruby raised her eyes.

'Ah, yes—silly question, I suppose.'

Moonlight stood on one leg outside Ruby's room, her hand on the wall for balance. She wore a black net skirt covered in sequins, gold wings attached to her waist, green tights and black satin ballet shoes, worn thin at the toes. She had The Parson with her, a spotted scarf round her neck. The Parson was making strange sucking sounds as she investigated a sore on her back leg.

'Philadelphia said you wanted me?'

'Can you dance?'

Moonlight lifted her left leg behind her, bent at the knee, twirled round twice, and then faced Ruby.

'I want you to dance when I play the accordion, out in the street, with people watching.'

'How much will you pay me?'

'Pay you?'

Moonlight fixed Ruby with her pale eyes, waiting.

'I'll pay you what you're worth in proportion to what we earn.'

'At least fifty pence?'

'I don't know. Oh all right then, at least fifty pence. I don't know how good you are yet.'

'Can I wear this?'

'You look weird.'

Moonlight's eyes widened. She sniffed.

'You look weird too actually.'

'This is my normal way of dressing.'

'I know.'

Moonlight continued to stare, until Ruby looked down at the dog.

'Why have you got The Parson?'

'She was wandering round on her own looking pathetic.'

Moonlight rose onto her toes again and brought her arms up over her head.

'Bring her too. Animals and children—guaranteed success.'

The front door opened and Willoughby returned from work. Ruby ran down to meet him.

'We're going busking. Please come with us. They're all coming except SA Pete, who's disappeared, sans the dog. I need you. I'll go mad if I'm alone with all these feckless Ducks.' She put her arms round his neck, but he took hold of her wrists and stepped away.

'Are you all right?' he asked.

'How all right? Of course I am.'

'You're kind of brittle. On edge.'

She pulled the band from her hair and shook it loose.

'Of course I'm brittle. That's why I have to do something before I break.'

'It's a mad idea, you know, with all the others.'

'Yes, yes, especially with Moonlight dancing instead of Gregor, but you have all night to draw, and I might never ask you to carry my accordion again. Who knows, something amazing might happen. Afterwards we'll have dinner at Antonio's. I can't bear it without you. Unless you come, I'll break into pieces like a china doll.'

'You're impossible.'

Willoughby carried Ruby's accordion to World's End, by the Salvation Army hut and the church. Philadelphia had dressed up in a lemon-yellow halter neck dress, and white sandals with very high heels. Birdy wore a skirt with a red poppy print and an orange tee shirt, and Monica, a silver tracksuit and pink trainers. They waited, lined up against the railings of the church. The Parson sniffed around like a stray.

Willoughby stood apart, reluctant to be part of the Gladstone Terrace audience, and too shy to stand close to Ruby and Moonlight. But, as Ruby began to play he forgot, for a moment, his awkwardness. Ruby—such vitality and delight. How could anyone pass by without stopping?

Moonlight stood, her arms held stiffly over her skirts. Taking tiny steps, she twizzled round on one foot and began to dance. People glanced, and looked away. Too tall to be sweet, her movements were gawky and graceless. Willoughby was afraid they would laugh at her, and then at Ruby too. He smiled in his nervousness, as if smiling would make everything all right.

He would draw later—the little group in their hodgepodge of clothing, and the strangers, who paused for a moment, then passed by. The clouds gathered and light rain began to fall. If only the rain would fall harder, and they could pack up and go home.

He felt Moonlight's vulnerability—he couldn't turn away. He watched her twirling round, head thrown back, the fabric wings waving on her back. He watched intently enough to see the transformation. Ruby's music shifted in tone and mood—she sang, words full of sweetness and longing. The child paused, her head inclined like a little dog. She began to move again, with pathos and delicacy, as if in a dream. She reminded him of Gregor as she turned to smile at Ruby. He felt a lump in his throat. He said Ruby's name quietly to himself.

He would always remember watching them, seeing that moment—a kind of miracle. Everything grotesque and pitiful about the child, became beautiful and extraordinary. He saw that Ruby recognised it too—she had created something, and, at the same time, she stood apart, like him, observing.

Alone in her room at night, Ruby opened the trunk where she kept her father's violin. She lifted it out and held it for a while, before unclipping the battered leather case. So precious—she hadn't touched it in the years she'd lived at Gladstone Terrace.

Are my hands like my father's, she thought? She had never wondered before what his hands looked like, or how the violin sounded as he played. He had been a wonderful musician—they had often said that. Her heart ached with longing for him.

Tenderly, she took the bow, tightened it and rubbed it with the aged block of rosin. She lifted the violin from its velvet nest, tuned each string and began to play—hesitant at first, full of shyness and awe. The dead come to us through music, she thought. There are no words, no other language. *I play for you, my Papa. Only you.*

They heard her; Moonlight glowing with success, awake in her bed, felt a lump in her throat, her eyes blinded by tears; Willoughby as he taped paper to his drawing board, preparing to draw Ruby and Moonlight. He stopped to listen. She played sensitively, exquisitely. Something had happened that afternoon, as he had known. They had all felt it—enchantment stealing over everything, so they each felt blessed in some subtle way.

It was impossible to think about drawing. Willoughby got up and stood at the window, looking out at the night sky as he listened. When it was quiet, he went down to her room. She had lit the candles on the mantelpiece.

'I knew you would come. Sleep with me, Willoughby. The world is full of bad things. But today something amazing happened and I want to hold onto it as long as I can.' She took his hand and led him to the bed. 'I'm so tired now, the room is spinning and the candles seem like great iridescent orbs. Do they seem like that to you too?'

She sank down and closed her eyes.

Willoughby had never stayed beside Ruby for an entire night. She slept curled on her side, her warm back pressed close. He put his arm round her, buried his face in the warm sweet scent of her hair. The candles guttered and burnt out and the headlights of passing cars streamed along the wall. He listened to her soft breathing. In his half-sleep he heard the front door open, footsteps on the stairs, the dog bark once. He opened his eyes to see Gregor's shadowy figure. Then he was gone, softly closing the door behind him.

Ruby stirred.

'Gregor. Despite everything, he still comes to see if I'm alive.'

'And are you?' he whispered.

She turned to face him; her face nestled into his neck.

'Do you find us very strange? Gregor and me?'

'Yes. And beautiful.'

'But you're strange too, so quiet, always watching people, and then going away and drawing. Sometimes it seems as if everyone in this house is floating through life, attached by invisible thread to something that just about keeps us alive. I think that *something* is Gregor's devotion to us all. I never realised until now. But it's become so fragile and precarious.'

She sat up, her eyes wide. 'I can't bear Gregor to go. What if he goes? It's not as if we're friends all the time. It's not about that. It's how he is, and I am, and everything that happened to us. I don't feel well when we're not together. I can't explain it, Willo.'

'What are you trying to say, Ruby?'

'I'm trying to explain.' She touched his lips with her fingertips, as if to quieten him.

He took her hand.

'It's all right. Don't explain. Better not. I know anyway.'

'You're kind to me. More than I deserve.'

She lay down and slept.

Willoughby gave up trying to sleep. He looked at her, knowing he would draw later—her face, beautiful in repose, hair tangled on the pillow, one hand, palm up, with fingers curled.

She was still asleep when he got up in the morning. He went down to the kitchen and found there was nothing for breakfast. The house was silent. He was glad of that, not wanting to meet anyone, wanting to keep her to himself for longer. He put on his clothes and went out to buy food.

When he returned, he made coffee and toast, fried bacon and eggs, and put everything on a tray to take up to her.

She'd just woken, and lay surrounded by cushions and silk bedding, staring at the ceiling. Seeing him with the tray, her face lit up.

'I bought breakfast,' he said. 'And these.'

He gave her a bunch of purple asters.

She reached for the flowers, buried her face in the thick of the blooms, as if drawing light from them. 'It's a miracle, Willo, you standing there with flowers and breakfast. I thought you'd left me, and I didn't know how to face the day. But you haven't. Fabulous.'

She slithered out of bed, and reached for a long silk dressing gown covered in roses from her wardrobe.

'First I must make myself beautiful. Then eat.'

As she moved, the edge of her dressing gown caught two sepia photographs on the trunk, so they slipped to the floor. Willoughby picked them up.

'Who is it in the photographs?'

'Oh those. I took them out of the trunk yesterday, with the violin. Gregor's mother, my Aunt Gitta. She was mad, Aunt Gitta, dragging Gregor from place to place in search of a dead Nazi.'

'Dead Nazi?'

'Gregor's father, my supposed uncle, who I'm glad I never met –Ernst von Loeben. Mama hated him.'

Standing by the light of the window, and holding a little mirror, Ruby checked her face, then brushed her hair and pinned it up.

'I only keep them so I don't forget. She called me an evil girl once. *Du bist ein boses Mädchen.*'

Willoughby looked intently at the images. Gitta, in the first photograph, was young, glamorous, sitting side-on to the camera, gazing over her shoulder, her silk dress falling perfectly down her back, the curls of hair in the nape of her neck.

In the other photograph, she stood on a beach with Ruby and Gregor. Ruby was still a child, and Gregor a teenager. Gitta's face was gaunt and haggard. Gregor's was full of anxiety, half turned to his mother, who looked down at the ground in an attitude of despair. Only Ruby stared directly at the camera, as if she considered smiling, and nearly managed. He was struck by the determination in her small vivid face.

'I am an evil girl.' She turned to look at him, shrugged. 'I don't care though.'

Gregor sat on the floor of Leda Godwin's living space, with the cassette recorder beside him. Leda sat opposite. The half empty brandy bottle stood on the table with their glasses. It was gloomy, but she hadn't switched on the light. Sometimes they sat for a long time without speaking, not registering the twilight, then darkness falling, until he got up to leave.

Often, before each session, Gregor felt that no words would come, that he had nothing left to tell her. Always he was wrong—in the quiet peace of her presence, a memory would surface, illuminate, until he had no choice but to speak. It sometimes seemed as if she drew his story out of the darkness.

I don't believe Johanne can have lived with us long, but those months were the happiest of my childhood, and when I think of Johanne, I feel warmth in my heart I try to do the same for everyone at Gladstone Terrace as she did for Mari and me. I can't. Never again, Leda. I can't bring her back.

It was different after we saw the prisoners that day. When I reflect back, it was as if we knew the bad times were accelerating, and we were being sucked into a vortex of destruction. This is not something you know with the mind. It's subliminal, and at the same time more visceral than that. Mari and Johanne sensed it, I'm certain, and through them I felt an uneasiness that made our time together more precious.

Mari and Johanne were rarely apart, and I tried in vain to be included. There was intensity about their closeness despite the age difference. I must have been tiresome. Their secrets made me more determined not to let them out of my sight.

Johanne's room, where she slept and was meant to go during her free time, was in the attic. But she said she hated being alone in that inhospitable house, so Mari and I would go up with her after dinner. I called it Johanne's lair—the safest place in the world. Mother never knew until that ill-fated night.

One cold spring day we'd been out in the gardens all afternoon. When night came we sat sleepy and contented by Johanne's stove. The table lamp was lit, and Mari and Johanne were sewing baby gowns from torn sheets—I knew not to ask. I'd constructed my own narrative that Johanne had a secret baby of her own. I leant over and admired their work, hoping they would tell me. When they said nothing, I went back to my book about the sea, dreaming of diving deep down to discover the creatures that lived in that mysterious world.

The door of Johanne's room was in a corner behind a wooden screen. Johanne had just put a log on the stove, so we didn't hear the door opening. I don't know how long Mother had been standing, half hidden by the screen, watching us. I looked up and saw her shadowy figure motionless in the corner of the room. I shot up and my book fell to the floor. Mari gasped. Mother's eyes darted from one of us to the other.

I'm reading about the sea—about the strange ocean creatures. I'm going to go diving one day, I said in a rush. Mari pushed her sewing down the edge of the chair.

The sea, Mother repeated, in a flat, disinterested voice. What are you both doing here, in the room of a servant?

Johanne isn't a servant, Mari said.

Mother turned to lock the door. Stand up, she commanded Johanne, moving forward so she loomed over her. What have you been teaching my children?

Johanne stood up and faced Mother. I teach as I was asked, Mrs von Loeben.

You've taken them walking.

You said we should go out for fresh air in the afternoons.

My daughter has been troubled by visions. Mother glanced at Mari-Louise, who flushed, and brought her hand to her face. You've deliberately exposed my children to danger.

Johanne didn't speak.

You know what I'm talking about. My husband told me you took the children into the city, taking a route by a work camp. The children afterwards were distressed by what they saw there. You're forbidden to take them out any longer.

But, Mummy, must we be shut in all day, like prisoners? All day, every day? Mari burst out.

You will do as I've instructed. You understand?

Johanne still said nothing. She looked directly at my mother.

There's another thing, my mother continued, her voice tremulous. Two nights ago my son refused to pray. He knelt in front of me, and would not open his mouth. How do you explain this?

Hitler is not God, Mama, I said, my voice squeaky with fear. Outside a gust of wind rattled the windowpanes. The clock began to chime. It was seven-thirty. We all waited until it stopped. She was so brave, Johanne Kuhn. She looked with her clear, direct gaze. She didn't flinch. It was Mother who wavered.

Miss Kuhn, you must understand the times we're living in. You have endangered my children. We will pray together now.

My mother drew nearer to us. Half lit by the lamp, dark shadows fell over her face, her eyes and the hollows of her cheeks. The plant on the bookshelf behind her looked weirdly as if it grew from her shoulders, great spiked leaves. My mother, who had no faith, demanded prayers.

Our personal beliefs are of no consequence, she whispered, her hand fluttering by her heart. I am married. My loyalty is to my husband and to my country. You appear not to understand that. All my life I've been surrounded by people who refuse to agree with me—my older sister, my father, now you, and what happened to them all? My sister had to leave the country and I've never seen her since—for all I know she might be dead. My father was only released from prison because my husband spoke up for him. He died soon afterwards, a broken man. I'm haunted by misfortune, and surrounded by enemies. What does it matter what I believe? But I will not have my children put at risk by these ideas you instil in them.

We're going to pray together, and ensure we're in agreement. We will say the Lord's Prayer, and then we will pray for the safety of our great leader. There can be no argument with that.

Mari looked in bewilderment at Johanne. No, Mama, she said.

I'm not a strong woman, Mother continued, a whine in her voice. Don't disobey me, please. It's only a prayer. I have no interest in religion, and our leader may just as well stand in for God. He is, after all, more real, more useful. God never answered a prayer of mine. Der Führer may well have more success. Now, kneel down. I'm ordering you.

I knelt and squeezed my eyes closed.

I will not, Mari said. She shook her head vigorously.

But Johanne knelt beside me, and took hold of Mari's hand.

Your mother is right, she said. We must do it now.

Mari put her arms round Johanne's neck, hiding her face from Mother.

Let go of Miss Kuhn Mari-Louise, you're being ridiculous. Repeat the words after me. Give our Führer, for his great work, your strength and power.

But we never said a word because at that moment the air raid siren began to wail, and for the first and only time, it was a relief.

The next morning after breakfast, Father came down and called Johanne into his office. Mari and I followed and waited outside his door, straining to hear what he said. After a long time he came out, locking the door behind him. He shouted for us to leave. He had business to do.

Mother said Johanne's mind was corrupted and her relationship with my sister was unhealthy. She refused to hear or speak any more about it. With a fixed smile, she opened her wardrobe door and made me choose a dress for her to wear that night. Her eyes glittered, as she held a blue satin gown to her chin. She turned this way and that.

I found Mari lying on the bed in Johanne's room. She had wrapped herself in Johanne's green woollen jersey, and she rocked as she wept. Everything else Johanne possessed had gone. Only the faint, yeasty smell of her lingered in the room. My poor sister. She wasn't even allowed to say goodbye. I lay down on the bed and put my arms round her thin shoulders.

After Johanne Kuhn left, silence settled over the house. Mari wandered from room to room, or gazed into the garden, her hands pressed against the windowpanes, waiting for the days to pass. I searched through picture books looking for something that might make her smile, but nothing broke through her despair. At mealtimes she would take tiny mouthfuls and say she wasn't hungry. I watched her turning the food over with her fork and pushing it to one side of the plate. She said food tasted like wool in her mouth. Nothing goes down when I swallow, she said, and put her hand to her throat.

Little love, I whispered, trying out the name Johanne had sometimes called her, hoping it would comfort her to hear. She looked up, her eyes full of tears. I'm not hungry, Gregor. Not hungry any more. Don't worry about me.

In sleepless nights, when the air raids didn't come, I sometimes heard her howling in her room. Please God help her to be happy, I prayed with urgency. Dear God, make her eat her dinner. I knew if she didn't she'd become too weak to run down to the shelter when the bombs came, and her feet would bleed like the prisoner girls. I waited, impatient for my prayers to be answered.

One morning a letter came from Johanne. Mari rushed upstairs to read it and I followed. She told me to leave her alone to think.

I left, one slow step at a time, down the stairs to my own room. I took the chess set out, but none of the characters, even the queens, wanted to play. Sick in my heart, I scattered them over the floor, trod on them and kicked them away.

There was a portrait of Hitler that hung in the bathroom—absurd though that seems. That evening Mari seemed different, as if Johanne's letter had renewed her strength. She turned Hitler to the wall, just as Johanne had once done, so der Führer couldn't watch us prepare for bed.

Hitler is an evil man, she said. Whatever Father says, we know that, and we must never forget it. We know it, don't we? She held my chin and looked closely into my face. It was like Mother staring at me, and I pushed her away. He's put a spell on the whole of our

135

country and nearly everyone in it. Our grandfather knew and that's why they sent him to prison. Johanne knew, and that's why they sent her away. I know too.

But you won't go away?

She shook her head. Then she covered her face with her hands and peered at me through her fingers. I think I'm very disobedient. I know there's no choice left.

Don't go away, I said again, in panic.

She filled the washbasin with water.

Let me wash you, she said, pulling me towards the water. She took the flannel and scrubbed it over my cheeks. When she dipped the flannel in the water again, I saw tears pouring down her cheeks, but she made no sound. Maybe, I thought, it's only her eyes that are sad. Her mouth isn't making a crying shape, so perhaps they're not real tears. I tried to convince myself things weren't really as bad as they seemed. I crept to bed and lay staring at the wall, listening for any sound in the house, waiting for the air raid siren, because even that would be a relief—it was no longer as frightening as my own sister had become.

Gregor fell into silence. Leda switched off the tape recorder. The tape had wound to the end. She put it into its case, dated it, and filed it in a box on her shelf.

'Gregor?' She whispered his name.

He turned to look at her.

'Are you there?' he said.

She knelt and took his hand. They lay, staring through the window at the darkening sky.

Ruby knocked on SA Pete's door. Hearing no answer, she went in. She found him kneeling slumped by his bed. He was wearing a grey tweed winter suit. His bald head shone in the summer twilight. An empty bottle of whisky was upturned on the floor. Beside the bottle—a revolver.

She gasped. 'Christ, Pete.'

He was drunk, unconscious. Heart racing, she picked up the revolver cautiously, as if it might accidentally fire in her hands. How terrible that he might have killed himself. She lifted his head from the bed. He grunted, but didn't open his eyes. She pulled the blanket from the bed and wrapped it round him, in case he was cold when he regained consciousness. She took the revolver to her room, poured herself a glass of port, drank it quickly, and poured another, until the shock subsided.

She held the revolver, felt the cold metal, the shape and weight of it against her soft hands. She hadn't realised how desperate SA Pete was. It could have been Gregor. If Gregor had found the revolver—she mustn't think of it. SA Pete should never have kept it in his room—he was a criminal. Anything could happen. She trembled, weak in every limb. She'd drunk too much port too quickly. The revolver must be hidden away whilst she decided what to do. She wrapped it in a silk camisole and unlocked the bottom drawer of her desk.

She hadn't opened the drawer for a long time. A scent of jasmine rose up from the paper drawer-liners she'd bought when she got married, and under the paper she knew she'd stowed a letter from Gregor. She felt for it with her fingers—Gregor's letter, written in 1961. She'd found it in her mother's desk, after Aunt Gitta had taken Gregor away for the last time—when she thought she'd never see him again. Oh, the strangeness of everything—the thought of SA Pete's revolver lying in the desk drawer next to Gregor's long-ago letter.

She put the revolver, in its silk wrap, on the floor. With the letter in her hand, she stood by the window, looking out at the pale blue sky. It had shaken her, seeing SA Pete slumped in his misery. Nothing and nobody could be relied upon. She spent her life trying to blank out that thought, but fear was always there, waiting for her guard to slip, waiting to torment her, as it did now. Leaning against the window frame, she sobbed.

A warm September afternoon, and Ruby was thirteen years old. They had gone to the sea—her mother, aunts and grandfather, with Aunt Gitta and Gregor. She and Gregor had run up the dunes, slithered down, and raced into the sea, under and over the waves, splashing each other and laughing. They swam far from the shore, hands locked together, treading water in the deep. *I love you, I love you,* Ruby sang. *I love you more than my heart. What does that mean? More than you can imagine.* Gregor had said that he loved her too, entirely. They smiled, seeing the sunlight dancing in each other's eyes.

Gitta walked over the sand, leaving Hedda and Aunt Marianne in the café. Gregor and Ruby heard her calling them from the water's edge.

'Leave her,' Ruby begged. 'You're always jumping at her call. Let's swim further out so we can't hear her.'

But Gregor couldn't. Suddenly chilled and shivering, they turned back.

Gitta took Gregor by the hand, even though he was no longer a child.

'We'll find your father,' she said. 'I believe we'll find him in eastern Germany. Yes, would you like that, Gregor? And when Mari-Louise returns to us, we'll be a real family again. It's all I want now.'

Gregor closed into himself, his face pinched and tight.

'But Mari-Louise has gone.'

'We have no proof of that. There was never any documentation from the hospital. We must hope. To give up hope is to admit defeat. You must never be defeated.'

Gregor pulled away from her, gathered up his clothes and walked off. When Ruby reached him, he was lost to her. It had been the happiest day, but Gitta had changed everything. *I love you more than my heart.* He couldn't look at her.

In the still, close evening, the dining table was perfectly set out, with white candles, silver cutlery and a bowl of yellow autumn roses. Everyone spoke in English out of consideration for Gitta, who understood very little Dutch. Marianne and Elise talked about the new plants they'd bought for the garden, and their piano pupils, and anything that was about nothing. They all felt the simmering tension, like electricity before a thunderstorm.

Gitta scarcely ate, but drank much wine. At the end of the meal, she announced, in German, that she would continue her search for Ernst for the rest of her life. Her gaze moved from one to the other round the table. Nobody spoke.

'You look at me with such disapproval, sister,' she said, her eyes resting with bitterness on Hedda. 'You will never know what we all suffered in Germany.'

'Nor will you ever know what it was like here,' Hedda replied, in English. For a moment she locked eyes with Gitta.

'To leave your country was your choice. You can't complain.'

Hedda got up to clear the plates.

'Why do you walk away?'

'Because there's nothing more to say to you, Gitta. It's all old ground. Let's not fight.'

She carried the plates out into the kitchen.

'I'll help,' Gregor said, and followed her out.

There was a brief silence. Nobody looked at Gitta. After a moment Grandmother asked Ruby to tell her about their day at the beach, she'd been so sorry not to be able to come.

'I see I'm being excluded,' Gitta said.

'No, not at all.' Elise touched Gitta's hand, in the sweet way she had. 'It's just, as Hedda said, all over now. We have to forgive and forget. We have to learn how to live again.'

'Oh you're all so sanctimonious,' Gitta said. 'Forget? I can't do that.' She pushed her chair away and left the room.

Elise flushed.

'Oh no, maybe that was the wrong approach.'

'My dear, everything you say will be wrong. Sadly Gitta is very unwell,' Ruby's grandfather said.

'Then I'm sorry I made it worse.'

In the kitchen they could hear raised voices as Gitta argued with Hedda.

'Germany got what it deserved,' Hedda said.

'That's a dreadful thing to say.'

'But nevertheless true. And if you find Ernst alive, he deserves to be hanged for everything he did. Why should he be spared?'

Gregor dumped the stack of plates in the sink and rushed out.

'I don't think Mother and Aunt Hedda are going to make friends,' Gregor said later to Ruby. 'Aunt Hedda thinks father was evil.'

'Was your father evil?' Ruby asked, sitting beside him on his bed.

'He did what everyone did. He served his country.'

Gregor went to the window. Hedda was pacing round the garden, smoking. In her bedroom, Gitta began to howl, a strange horrific sound, like an animal in pain. Gregor and Ruby looked at each other.

'I should go to her,' Gregor said. 'I know this noise. It's terrible for her.' His face was tight with misery.

'Do you want to?'

'No. I want to run away. I'm torn in pieces.'

Ruby clung to him.

'I'll hold you together, with all my strength, all my life. I promise, Gregor, I promise.'

'I don't think you can. I don't think anyone can.'

Gitta locked herself in her room and wouldn't let anyone in. Hedda, grey and exhausted, walked with Gregor and Ruby down to the river café. They sat under the golden-leaved willow trees and floated sticks in the water. They drank coffee. Hedda hummed quietly, a melody she often sang. Gregor picked the rushes that grew by the water's edge, and Ruby filled a basket with blackberries.

'You look so sad, Aunt Hedda.' Gregor put his arms round her shoulders.

She sighed and leant the back of her head against his chest. 'Look after each other,' she said. 'You're good children—though not really children any more. You're so much better than we all deserve.' She smiled.

The next day Gregor and Gitta left. Nobody knew where they had gone.

Ruby wandered around the house at night. Her heart was broken. She drifted from room to room, until sorrow was anaesthetised by exhaustion.

She opened the door of her grandfather's surgery, closed it quietly behind her and stood in the darkness, listening to the silence of the night, sensing the edges of the furniture. When she turned on the lamp the first thing she saw was the plaque on the wall—words written in fine black ink and framed in oak.

The physician's highest calling, his only calling, is to make sick people healthy—to heal.

She spoke the beautiful words aloud. *To make sick people healthy—to heal.* Her kind wise grandfather, who had lived through so much sadness. He would know how to heal her broken heart.

She sat in his chair, put her head down on the arm and cried herself to sleep. She woke as the door opened. It was morning, and he had just come into the room.

'Little Dora. What are you doing here?' He looked down at her and touched her cheek.

'You're a doctor,' she said, opening her eyes.

The reverential tone in her voice made him smile.

'I was. But I know very little, even so.'

'You're old and wise. You must know.'

'After all these years perhaps I should, and yet the more I see, the more baffling life becomes. But what are you doing, my chicken, here in my study so early?'

'I was too sad to sleep. I wandered around and found myself here. I miss Gregor so much, Grandfather. My heart is broken. I hate Gitta for taking him away.'

She started to cry again. He drew up a chair beside her and took her hand.

'We must try to forgive her, try to forgive your aunt Gitta. She's lost everything, her husband and daughter, and her home.'

'You lost my papa but it doesn't make you cruel. She said I was an evil girl. She came into my room two nights ago, and stood over my bed and said it, in German but I knew what she said.'

He held her hand firmly. He was slow to speak.

'She's a very sick woman, sick in her mind, Dora. You're not an evil girl. You know that.'

'I don't care if she is sick. She's taken Gregor. She'll fill his heart with horrible things. She'll take away his happiness. She'll destroy him.'

'Don't let her hurt you too, darling.'

She covered her eyes with her hands, and thought, *I'll shut her out. I'll make the biggest commotion. I'll learn how to play every musical instrument in the world. I'll sing at the top of my voice until I can't hear her voice any more. Until she's dead.*

Ruby leant against the window, looking out at the sky. The breeze had streaked the thin white clouds into mares' tails. She closed her eyes, opened them again, took Gregor's letter from the envelope, and read.

Dearest Aunt Hedda,

I will come back to you. Tell Dora I won't fail you. Even if it takes an age, by train and horseback, or walking, if I have to. Whatever it takes, I will come home, where I belong with you.

We're in Germany again, as you will see from the postmark. This is where Mother wanted to come to continue her search for Father. She holds to the belief that he was a good man, and insists he's wandering somewhere in Eastern Germany, suffering from amnesia, unable to find his way home. She writes letters to unknown people asking for help. I don't want him back. The thought frightens me.

I'm glad that you taught me English so well. I try to think in English. I buy English books when I can, and put them under my bed, in the hope they'll drift into my dreams. Dora would tease me if she knew. I should dance, for that needs no words. I will grow old and no longer speak. I'll dance with all my heart, like you.

It's a full moon tonight and I stand and think of you under the same sky, the same moonlight, in our house on the edge of the forest. The tree outside my room here is stark and sad; the branches have been cut, leaving only the trunk. I feel like the tree, trying to grow new green leaves out of the mutilation.

This is my address, for now at least. Thank you for your letters in advance. I will carry them with me in the pocket of my jacket and take them out to read and find comfort. You, of all people, know how hard it is, the terrible guilt of it all.

There is a dreadful silence; we see no devastation, we pretend it isn't there and that nothing happened. We can't speak of the evil we allowed to grow.

Dearest Aunt Hedda and Dora, I love you both with all my heart. I will return when Mother no longer needs me so very badly.

Your Gregor.

Ruby held the letter, gazed down at Gregor's tiny writing, the faded blue ink. She folded it, and tucked it down the front of her dress.

Who else was in the house—Willoughby out at work, Moonlight at school, Gregor, gone wherever he went these days. The others would be somewhere in the house.

She had to do something for SA Pete. On impulse, she tore a sheet of paper from a notebook in her bag. *I'm certain Jesus loves you*, she wrote. She took the message down to his room. He slept, breathing heavily. She tucked the note under his limp hand, and left a pint glass of water in place of the revolver.

Back in her room, she looked at the revolver nestled in cream satin and lace, and wondered if it was loaded. What should she do with it? Nobody would know if it remained covered up in her drawer. She could take it out from time to time; pop it in her bag—the one decorated with the bunch of plastic flowers—and wander around chatting to people. Nobody would know she had the power to kill at her fingertips.

How would that feel? Her father had known. During those years in Holland, he would have carried a gun.

If she'd had a gun, and if she'd been commissioned to sing or play for Hitler, would she had drawn the gun and shot him? If Hitler had been shot, would another Hitler have taken his place? She felt a buzzing in her head, like wasps.

She thought, I can take the revolver and walk to Leda Godwin's warehouse. She won't know what's hidden in a bag decorated with a bunch of plastic flowers. Afterwards, it will be a story that everyone will remember for years.

It had clouded over. A fine rain fell—she could see though the window. Her sense of the absurd faded away. She tucked the revolver away, closed the drawer, and went down to the kitchen.

Monica was making toast. Crumbs were scattered over the floor and the workbench, the bread was cut haphazardly in great chunks. Philadelphia was slumped at the kitchen table, smoking, and drinking orange juice with aspirin.

'Oh, I'm so tired,' she said, and lolled her head onto her folded arms.

'You're always unhappy or tired. There's nothing to be tired and unhappy about. Nothing is any different from any other day, is it?' Ruby snapped. 'Do something instead of flopping around.'

'You're so unkind. You're not like Gregor.'

'No. Be thankful for that. If you think I'm unkind then move out. I'm sure there are plenty of kind people waiting to house you.' She sat down beside Philadelphia and took one of her cigarettes from the packet on the table. 'I don't mean that, as you must know. I like to fill the house with mad people. It makes me seem normal. Give me a light. I want to ask you something.'

Philadelphia handed her the box of matches.

'You as well,' Ruby said, addressing Monica. 'You can answer, too, after you've finished demolishing the bread. The question is—what would you do if there was someone you felt haunted by, someone you were desperate to be free of? How would you go about getting free of them? Tell the truth.'

Philadelphia pushed her hair back and sat up.

'The only time I ever sent someone packing I wanted him back again as soon as he'd gone,' she said. She stubbed out her cigarette in a cracked saucer. Her long hair fell on either side of her face again. 'I think that's the problem I have. I love too much.'

'That's not helpful. You've told us many times about the absent lover. I'm looking for fresh perspectives. Monica? What answer can you give?'

Monica was wearing a blue quilted dressing gown; her plump feet were encased in fur-lined slippers. Her eyes were oddly illuminated as she turned to Ruby. She held the bread knife in her hand.

'There are plants that will kill—deadly nightshade, chopped up, mixed with raspberries and put in a jelly.'

'Poison, like a rat?'

'You leave a fruit jelly in a glass bowl in the fridge, with a note saying *please eat me*. In that way, nobody can say you've committed murder.'

Ruby stared at Monica.

'I think you'd find that they might.'

'You said I could give any answer.' Monica's eyes glazed over for a moment, then she giggled. 'I read it once.'

'You look so ordinary, Monica. How looks deceive.'

'There are consequences,' Philadelphia said. 'Whatever you do, good or bad, there are always consequences, and that's what you have to live with.'

Ruby found SA Pete later, slumped in a grey towelling dressing gown just above the turn in the stairs, head bowed.

'What are you doing sitting there in your bath robe?' she called down.

He turned, startled.

'I didn't know you were there, Ruby. You're so light on your feet. I just took a bath.'

'But didn't quite make it back to your room?' She ran down to sit on the step above him. Will he say anything, she wondered? 'Where have you been all this time? You missed seeing me busking and Moonlight dancing.'

'I'm sorry about that.' He blinked and looked at her, as if emerging from a dream and trying to focus. 'I've been in my own world.'

He looked slightly unhinged. She was glad she'd hidden his revolver.

'It's a miracle.' His face was earnest, no sense of irony in his tone. 'I had a very bad day, worse than ever, as if a light went out, and I couldn't see a way to put one foot in front of the other. I hated myself. I thought it was the end. I guess you don't know what I'm talking about? Why should you?'

'But maybe I do, Pete.' She put her hand on his shoulder.

'I should have said. I know that. It was often on the tip of my tongue, but my courage would fail. I'm telling you now. In the drawer by the bed in my room, I keep a revolver. It was my father's. I should have handed it in, but I couldn't let go. I see that now. I never thought of the risk, Ruby. I promise.

'I'd had a bit to drink, and wasn't thinking straight. I went to the drawer and took the revolver out. I heard a voice in my head saying *go on shoot yourself, you worthless nothing. You'll be better off dead.*

'I thought of the temptation of Our Lord. I wanted sweet relief, Jesus, how I longed for it. I knelt to pray.

'A miracle happened, Ruby. I can only see it as a miracle. I fell asleep before I could hold the gun to my head. I fell into the deepest sleep.

'When I woke up, everywhere was lit up with golden light– the sky, the walls of my room, the windows. I had no headache, no desperation. With prayers on my lips, I reached for the revolver to put it back safely in the drawer. But it had gone, and in its place I found a piece of paper and a few words of love. I'd forgotten, like the lost sheep. The words brought me back.'

They sat quietly a moment. The sun streamed through the window. Silver dust motes floated through the light. Ruby put her hand over his.

'Perhaps someone found you, took the revolver away, saved you from yourself?'

'I've wondered that. If so, it was an act of great kindness. I don't ask to know who it was.'

Laughter bubbled inside her, a sudden joy. The revolver incident had been a marvellous distraction. If only she could tell someone.

'Good things happen sometimes, Pete.'

'I think I should move on, find a new direction in life, start to take some responsibility.'

'Responsibility is much overrated, you'll find. Do you want coffee? I was going to make some, but your marvellous story distracted me.'

'I'd like coffee. I wish I knew where the revolver had gone,' he added as an afterthought.

'There's a word for it—transmogrified.' She tried to hold her laughter, but it exploded from her. 'Sorry Pete, it's just relief that you're not dead. The revolver transmogrified into words of love. Don't question your miracle. Just believe it.'

I'm in a mad house she thought, as she made coffee. If only someone could make a miracle happen for Gregor. If I sleep, like SA Pete did, will I wake and find everything changed—the golden light of sunrise, angels, a handwritten note of love, and Gregor smiling over breakfast?

The way Leda sat as she listened had become familiar to Gregor—one hand on the desk in front of her, the other arm over her thin chest. She had a way of always looking chilly, even on the warm summer days. To Gregor, her eyes seemed very dark, a fathomless dark. Who is she, why do I trust her? Over a few weeks she'd become more to him than an ordinary woman, theatre director, artist, friend, or anything else she professed to be. I love her, he thought, startled by the realisation. I love her without even knowing who it is I love. Tears filled his eyes. I will be able to tell her everything. I will be released from it all at last.

'Leda...,' he wanted to say something, to profess his love, but he couldn't find the words.

'Tell me what you can,' she insisted, in her quiet way. 'Anything, everything you remember.'

'Everything, yes—the children's nursery in the birch woods, the end. The end... Why did Mari take me with her that day? Where was that terrible place, what was it about?'

'You could still find out,' Leda said. 'If nothing else, the Germans have always been meticulous in their record-keeping.'

'Find out? It was...' He blinked, drew his hand over his eyes. 'The truth might be unbearable.'

He reached for the glass of water and drank. 'I'm very cold.' He started to shake. 'I remember now.'

The shadow of a bird crossed the window, dark commotion of beating wings.

'A magpie,' Leda said, catching his glance. 'One for sorrow. It's cold. I'm sorry—so cold here after rain. Do you want to leave it today?'

He shook his head.

'No let's go on.'

Mari woke me early one Sunday. Father was in a meeting all day. Mother had been awake in the night, and said we mustn't disturb her. I can't leave you here alone, Mari told me. I'm meant to stay here and look after you, but it's very important that we go to Johanne. Johanne and I will do our work, and you will stay with the old mother, like you did the last time. You'll be all right, Gregor, won't you? I argued that I wanted to go with her and Johanne. I didn't want to stay with the old mother. But you must, my darling, and afterwards everything will be better. We can make plans for the future. She was a little excited, almost happy that morning. She never called me darling again.

It was nice to go on the streetcar again, though everywhere had changed since the air raids had begun. I looked from the window, saw staircases that led nowhere, and bedrooms hanging in space, and wondered how the poor people moved all their furniture when they went to look for a new house. We were fortunate to be rich and to live out of town, away from the factories and steel foundries.

We got down from the streetcar and crossed the cemetery, half running, not daring to look at the barbed walls and the iron gates of the prison camp. I could tell Mari was overjoyed at the thought of seeing Johanne again, and eager to get there. I was too. I had an idea we could leave home and live with her, and I was making plans in my head. It would be wonderful. But when we reached her house and knocked, nobody answered. Mari tried the door. It was locked.

It's very strange, she said. Johanne's mother is never away. Has she been taken ill, and where is Johanne? She said to come. She said so in her letter, Gregor. And now all the shutters are down. Oh, I don't know what to do. What shall I do?

I was overcome with a dreadful sensation, as if my heart had fallen into a dark empty place. An eerie ringing sounded, was it in my head, or coming from outside me? I tried to speak, but I couldn't open my mouth. I could hardly breathe.

A man emerged from the next house. He was thin, and sour looking, a streak of soot across his forehead, his damp grey hair plastered to his skin. He leant against the doorframe of his house, and tapped the heel of his boot on the stone step. He stared at Mari, his eyes scanning her face, taking in her birthmark. A chicken clucked loudly in the yard—there was a scuffle, a flapping of wings.

She won't be back, he said. He looked at Mari, his eyes greedy for her reaction. They know how to deal with traitors. None of that lot will be back. Let's say that they've gone on their holidays, a one-way ticket. He grinned and ran his tongue over his lips. I'll be looking after things from now on.

We ran, Mari's breath fast and desperate, as if she was drowning. I stumbled and called out, struggling to keep up. She turned, grabbed my wrist and dragged me with her.

When, at last, we reached an area of woodland, and she stopped, my legs trembled with exhaustion and I collapsed, face down, on the earth. The pale sun filtered through the golden birches. The fallen leaves, like golden discs, floated in pools of rainwater.

Can we go home? I asked.

We can't, not yet. She knelt beside me, her face very close. I felt somehow disembodied. I tried to hear what she said through the roaring waves in my ears.

I'm going to the nursery, where the babies of the prisoners are taken. Johanne promised the Polish girl we would go because she can't.

Why can't she?

The guards don't allow mothers to visit their children. It's a new regulation. Don't you understand, Gregor?

Mari pulled me up and led me along a twisting sandy path through the woods. We stopped where the trees thinned out.

You must wait here until I come back. Wait here. Don't move.

But I want to see the babies too.

No, she whispered. It's not a good place. Stay here. Please wait for me. I have to go on my own.

I looked down at the ground. I couldn't bear to look at her eyes. Everything seemed so fragile and insubstantial. That terrible empty place still rang in my head. She made me sit under a tree and she collected leaves into a pile and told me to make a picture by pressing them into the earth. I wanted to help her, so I tried to obey.

I'll be back very soon.

But it wasn't soon. After a long time I kicked away my leaf pattern. The sunlight had moved to another part of the woods and the air became cold and damp. I kept looking along the path through the trees where she'd disappeared from sight, so long ago, hoping she'd suddenly appear—but nothing, nobody, only squirrels, crows with their lonely cries, and small flies disturbing the air.

I counted my steps so I'd know how to return to the same place. After I'd walked for seven hundred and sixty four steps along the path, I reached a long concrete building with rows of barred windows. It was a kind of army barrack. I think there was more than one building, but I only saw the first. I was certain this was where Mari had gone.

The double doors were open. I didn't have any fear, despite the hostility of the place—my strongest desire was to find Mari. I went into a cold white lobby. The smell made me gag and hold my nose— disinfectant, sour milk, vomit. I heard the piercing cries of infants from above, and I kept on, past a room where an old grey woman sat knitting, and up a narrow stairway to a room that ran the length of the building. This room was full of metal cots in long rows, and lights with green shades dangling from the ceiling. In every cot there was a baby. They cried, or whimpered, or lay still. They were very thin. They were sick, Leda. Row on row of sick, dying babies—the stench of it, the terrible sound.

My sister was there, holding a baby in a bundle of rags close to her body, her head bent low. When she looked up her eyes didn't seem to see me.

Everything went dark, an explosion in my head, a bright, clear light. I could breathe again. I knew Mari loved the creature she held. I knew I had to love it too.

You shouldn't have come, Mari whispered. I told you not to. He's very sick. I don't know what to do. There are no doctors. They say everything is under control.

I touched the limp cold hand. The baby's eyes were huge in the tiny wrinkled face. He looked straight at me. An overwhelming need to do something rushed in. It was the end of everything—there was nothing beyond this moment. I knelt beside Mari so my breath fell on the infant's cheek. In my head the words came, but I didn't voice them—do you want milk, or is it just a little rock to sleep? Or do you want to go out into the fresh air? We'll do whatever you need. We'll take you home with us and look after you. I was filled with a sense of purpose. Mari sank down to sit on the floor, cradling the child on her lap, and I squatted beside her. We stroked the tiny body as it arched and convulsed, and a thin white fluid dribbled from its mouth. I stroked, not knowing the baby had died.

Mari cried out as if she'd been struck. She shook the baby with desperation.

Footsteps struck the floor, hard, fast, and coming towards us. I clutched Mari and dared not look up. I had the notion that the solid stocking-clad legs I stared at and the feet that wobbled in tight black shoes, were made of polished wood. The person with the wooden legs snatched the baby and bundle of rags, and threw him back into the cot.

What are your names? Where do you come from?

She took us to a room and made us wait. There were no windows in the room. A portrait of der Führer smiled down. Somewhere, quite near, we heard Wooden Legs speaking on the telephone, her voice angry, indignant, as if she'd been wronged. I held Mari's hand.

Everything is over, she said, her voice toneless. She kept saying it. *It's over now. He is dead. The baby is dead.* Spasms shook her body.

A man arrived in a car and we were let out of the airless room. The man spoke to the woman. Their voices were cold and sharp, and the words made no sense to me. The man's lips were tight, and he gripped Mari's shoulder and my arm and pushed us into the car, slamming the door, nearly trapping Mari's leg. I still held her hand, as if that would help. I knew nothing would help. We had to get to the end of our lives, endure everything until it was over.

Father came out to meet the car. He didn't speak. He put us in his office and locked the door. We both wanted to go to the toilet, but there was nowhere to go. I wet my trousers, but it didn't matter this time. Mari tried to wipe the puddle with paper from the desk, but it didn't work. She gave up and sat staring down at the floor.

We didn't turn on the lights. It got dark in the room. When Father returned and switched on the lamps, the glare of light was a *shock. Father's face was flushed, his hands big and red, his voice very strange. He wanted an explanation.*

The baby was sick and hungry, Daddy. I tried to save him. Mari's voice came out high-pitched and strange.

Father stepped back and observed her from a distance.

All the children—they just cry and want to be held, but their mothers can't come to them. They're in the prison. Her words rushed out.

Don't garble, he said.

She swallowed. Her voice kept catching in her throat. His number was 23. Boy, number 23, a Polish mother. We tried to save him for her. Johanne cuddled him and said how one day his mummy would come. One day. We made clothes for him. We made clothes, Daddy, please help.

You were told to look after Gregor. So the sick baby of a Polish labourer means more to you than your own brother?

She cried.

I was fine, Daddy, I whispered. I went to help the babies too.

Father carried on speaking. You're sick. Poor Mari-Louise. Sick, just like your mother. What am I going to do? I should punish you, shouldn't I? Tell me, how should I punish you?

Mari-Louise closed her eyes. She seemed scarcely to breathe. She wouldn't speak. He paced around her, staring down. Speak, he kept saying. When she wouldn't, it was as if something in him broke, He started to beat her with his fists.

Don't hurt her Daddy. Don't hurt her.

I screamed. My screaming filled my whole body. I had no control. I can't remember what happened.

Merciful God—did I stop my father hurting her? She was so small and fragile, Leda. So small and fragile and brave.

For many years, after Hitler was dead, when I lived in Amsterdam, and later in England, I would wake up in the morning and say— today my sister will come. I didn't know how that could be, but I was certain. Perhaps she'd arrive on the last train, or there'd be a letter from someone who had news of her. But I never found her or discovered anything about what happened. I think about her every day. I don't hope any longer that I'll ever see her again. Would I even know her if she walked into this room? It's thirty years ago. What would she look like now?

After the incident with the baby I was made to stay day and night with my mother, to eat and sleep with her. Where's Mari? I kept asking. She's sleeping. Always sleeping. She's very tired. The only times I could get free of Mother were when the air raid sounded. I thought Mari would come down to the cellar when the sirens started. But instead Mother made me go down with the servants. She said she would rather die than be buried alive. She pushed me out of her room and turned the key. Where's my sister? I asked the servants. The two women who did the cooking looked at each other. She's in hospital, the old one said.

Plans were made for me to go to a safe place—to my grandmother in the country. Will Mari come with me, I asked? But Mother told me procedures were in place for Mari's safety and, as she was very sick, she couldn't come with me to Grandmother. When she's better she'll join you. I was told I must be well behaved and give no trouble to my grandmother, who was a frail old lady.

I lived with my grandmother in two small cold rooms, with a view of a dense green hedge through the window. My uncle was away, fighting. We heard the planes at night, but they went over, beyond us, to the city, and Grandmother said we could sleep easily in our beds because the bombs wouldn't fall in the village. I didn't love my grandmother.

I asked every morning, where my sister had gone. Mari-Louise has gone on her holidays, she said. Her lips were tight and she wouldn't look at me. I knew she wasn't telling the truth. Will she come today? Not today. Tomorrow? Possibly. In the morning I'd stand by the window, watching people pass, hoping to see a car draw up, and my sister's pale face in the window. Nobody came.

I have no memory of any kind of school, and the days are long in my mind. We played cards together in the afternoons. I tried to do as she asked, to be good. Every day I felt I was getting smaller.

Winter came—dark wet days, and then spring, summer, another autumn. How long was I there? I have no idea. In the morning I was allowed to walk to a little park where I sat on a bench and watched the leaves falling. I counted the days by drawing dots on the wall next to my bed. I made the dots into grids.

One day I had the strongest feeling that my father was nearby. I went to the window, and sure enough, I saw him walking towards the house. I waited, my heart thumping. When he arrived, my grandmother told me she needed to speak to him alone. They told me to wait, and closed and locked the door. Sick at heart, and trying not to cry, I drew a picture of an angel holding a baby. I drew it for my sister, so he could take it to her.

My father came to where I sat alone. He stood in the doorway watching me. I wanted to rush to him, but something made me freeze. We looked at each other across the room, and for a while neither moved. He came to me, put his hand on my head.

We will all be together again soon, when Germany has defeated the enemy, he said.

When? When will that be? My voice quavered. I hugged myself.

Very soon, he said.

I gave him my drawing for Mari-Louise and asked him to bring a photograph of her the next time he visited. I had no photograph. I had nothing of hers. I asked him to bring her gloves, the furry ones I so loved the feel and smell of. And I would imagine the touch of her hand on my cheek.

He looked down at the drawing and chewed his lip. I thought he was crying. But fathers don't cry. He folded my angel and put it in his pocket. I have been plagued with bad luck, he said, turning to look at me. I saw then that he was crying. I felt my own heart breaking. Mari-Louise is in hospital.

Will they make her better?

They will look after her. We must try to forget what happened.

I put my arms round his waist.

Take me home, Daddy. Please take me home. I can't bear it here. I want to go home.

What am I to do, Gregor? I haven't been a good father, to you or your sister. Now, I'm afraid it's too late. Forgive me. An uncontrollable madness takes over. I've never been the person I want

155

to be. He fell to his knees and held me close to his chest. *My son, my son*, he said. I felt I'd suffocate.

He got up abruptly, and in a few moments, before I could take in what was happening, he'd gone. I rushed to the window and saw him walking away. He didn't turn back. I lay face down on the floor and howled into my hands so Grandmother wouldn't hear.

I had those terrible dreams of dancing on the table after that. It always started with me standing on a high table surrounded by men in Nazi uniform. They asked me to do tricks, to make them laugh, because laughter was in such short supply since the humiliation of Germany. Those words came so clearly in my dreams— *humiliation of Germany*. *Pull a monkey face, dance on your toes.* They applauded and laughed. *Smoke a cigar*—someone pushed it between my teeth, into my mouth and I coughed. *He makes a great little man*, they said, *a proper little Nazi boy.*

Then I saw my father, thin and exhausted, standing at the door watching me. *My son, my son.* He stretched his hands, Christ-like, towards me. I started to run towards him. I always woke before I fell into his arms.

Gregor stopped. Somewhere in the building someone was playing the piano, perhaps for a ballet class. Such an ordinary and lovely thing it seemed to him, and he closed his eyes to listen.

Leda turned the cassette off, and went to him, rested her hand on his shoulders. He heard her breath, felt it through her hand, falling, rising, and didn't want to move.

It had rained all the time he'd been speaking, but now the sun emerged from a white sky, and the river gleamed in the space between the buildings.

Is it over? Have I any more to tell her? He opened his eyes.

'The morning I left my grandmother's house I woke with a start. I felt a vibration in my head. I still have that feeling sometimes, so powerfully it distances me from everything, and nothing seems real. I knew that if I didn't leave her house I would die. Taking only a few things with me, I went down before she was up, opened the door and crept out. I begged a lift on a cart. My plan was to go to the train station, then back to the city to find Mari-Louise.

'After that everything is blank. I believe an air strike must have happened. I remember so little, how many weeks or months until it was over? I don't know.

'I lived in a cellar. There were other people.

'I survived. I never saw my grandmother or my father again.

'Mother said Mari had been taken to hospital. To hospital. What kind of place was it? What did they do to her?

'There's nothing left to tell you. I'm so tired.'

Willoughby drew in the long light evenings through the summer when the house was quiet, when Ruby was out modelling for her class, or gone to seek company in Antonio's. He was engrossed in the faces that seemed to emerge from the blank paper, and drew as daylight faded. He didn't hear Ruby on the stairs, or sense her watching from the doorway until she said his name. He turned. She was carrying a candle.

'I didn't want to bring too much light to the man who works in the dark, so here I am, by candlelight. I have to see if you're still drawing Gregor's alter-ego.'

She put the candle down beside the easel and scrutinised his work—the same face he drew every night from different angles—a young man with large heavily lidded eyes, hair swept back clean from a narrow forehead.

'Ah yes, here he is. Gregor in essence, but not Gregor at all in the shape of his head, or eyes, or any feature really. It's uncanny. Do you see the face in your mind's eye before you make a mark?'

'Not consciously, all the seeing is in my hands. That's how it seems anyway.'

'It's weird, the way this same face keeps emerging from nowhere.'

'It doesn't feel weird to me.'

Ruby scanned the room. He had taped all the drawings to the wall.

'That one is like the bloody Mona Lisa, looking at me wherever I go. Disturbing.' She put her hands over Willoughby's eyes. 'Please stop, just for a minute. I've got a question,' she said, repeating what she'd asked Philadelphia and Monica.

'I would leave.' He took her hands and knotted his fingers with hers. 'I would go far enough away so I wouldn't have to see them again.'

'If it wasn't possible to go away, what would you do then?'

'I would leave in my mind. I wouldn't think of them any longer, until in the end they might as well be invisible.'

'Is your mind really that strong?'

'I believe so.'

'Whatever we do, good or bad, there are always consequences. We have to be able to live with the consequences.'

They looked into each other's eyes longer than they ever had. The intimacy made his heart quicken, and he blushed.

'If I go out to the Greek shop for baklava, will you stop drawing then?'

'You're bribing me to stop. You don't need to bribe me, Ruby.'

It was dark when Ruby walked back with her basket of provisions to share with Willoughby—a bottle of cheap port, Stilton cheese and crackers and baklava. She hummed quietly, and thought of the night ahead, how nice it would be—with Willoughby in bed, then drinking and listening to music. It would be a distraction from Gregor's misery and the thought of SA Pete's revolver. Glancing up, she saw that all the lights were on in the house. That was unusual. Either Moonlight had left them on in her fear of the dark, or Gregor was home at last from his night walks? But Gregor always crept in like a fugitive, so it couldn't be him. She opened the front door, stepped in, put her shopping down, and stood listening under the glittering chandelier. Gregor was on the top floor landing.

'I need witnesses, where's Ruby? Where's SA Pete? I need everyone here, now.' His voice was raised, agitated.

Ruby ran up the stairs. Willoughby met her halfway, put his hand on her arm.

'Ruby, listen,' he tried to stop her going up.

'What? What's going on? Has there been an accident?' She pushed past him and went on up the stairs.

Gregor was calling for everyone to come to Willoughby's room. She thought, he's been drinking, but he never gets drunk. Why now? Bewildered and nervous, because he was so unlike the man they knew, they emerged from their rooms—Philadelphia like a goddess, her hair down, wearing a yellow and orange kaftan, Moonlight in a white lace nightdress she'd almost grown out of, the sisters in their fur-lined slippers and quilted dressing gowns. At least Willoughby and SA Pete were dressed, Pete still in his dark suit as if he'd attended a funeral. Thank God the dog isn't here too, Ruby thought. At which point The Parson trotted out, and gazing up at Moonlight, wagged her tail.

'It's not inconsequential,' Gregor said, looking around at everyone. 'I need you all to see this. I need you to hear me. This is no accident, I must stress.'

He led them into Willoughby's room where the light of the lamp was focussed on the easel.

'You've drawn a portrait of my father,' he said, turning to Willoughby. 'Not only one portrait, but many. When and where did you meet him? Where is he now?'

'You know that's not possible, Gregor,' Ruby said.

'Be quiet, for once, Ruby.' Gregor made a grand gesture, like an actor, towards the easel, and then around the room where the other drawings were pinned. 'Come in, don't crowd round the door,' he commanded. 'Look. My father is everywhere, staring down at me, at all of us. This is exactly the way he wore his hair, the way he held his head. All that's missing is his uniform, the Nazi badge of allegiance.' He put his hand to his mouth. 'It disturbs me greatly. You, Willoughby Stone, are you possessed by my father?'

'Possessed? Can't you see the drawings are meant to be you? I've drawn everyone in this house, you can look through my sketch books if you want proof.' Willoughby spoke calmly. 'You happen to be the most difficult to draw.'

'How did you meet my father, Ernst von Loeben? Where did you meet him? Where is he now?'

'Look, man, I've never even been to Germany, or anywhere else abroad for that matter.'

Gregor's eyes met Willoughby's. Willoughby shrugged, made a slight gesture of surrender with his hands.

'Nevertheless, my friend, my father must have visited you in dreams, because here he is. And now you will all sit down, somewhere in this room, if Willoughby Stone will allow us to intrude on his gallery. You must listen to me.'

'You're welcome,' Willoughby said in exasperation. 'Sit here Birdy.' He pulled up chair, and invited the others to perch on his bed and on cushions on the floor.

Gregor, his face flushed and eyes bright, turned to the window and pressed his forehead against the glass, waiting. They sat down, not daring to look at each other.

'That is my father without any doubt.' Slowly he turned back to look at them all. 'Am I guilty? You're the judge, Willoughby. You have judged me from the first. You stand apart, watching us. You sit in your room making these drawings. What are they for? What evidence do you need? Oh, I mean no offence. I like you. But still, you set yourself apart like a judge.'

He stood before the easel, put out his hand and touched the portrait.

'My father was so sweet that day. It seemed to me that he must be a kind, good person after all.'

Nobody spoke. Birdy smiled in bewilderment. Monica watched, goggle-eyed. SA Pete bowed his head and prayed. Philadelphia blinked back her tears, and Moonlight pulled at her fingers until her knuckles cracked. Willoughby leant against the wall, his hand on Ruby's shoulder. She stared down at the floor, seemed scarcely to breathe.

'Father was so very sweet and kind that day,' Gregor repeated. 'He wanted to know about my sister's companion, Johanne Kuhn. I told him Johanne was kind and funny and made us laugh. I didn't tell him about the way Johanne talked of der Führer. I didn't actually tell him that, I'm certain. I didn't, did I? Oh God, unbearable, unbearable. Did I betray them both? Father was unusually interested in me, affectionate, so I told him of our visits to Johanne's family and how Johanne and Mari would leave me with the old mother. I told him that I didn't know where they went with their baskets full of baby clothes.

'Was it a dream, or did that incident in the factory really happen the same day? The day Father was so kind? Why did I trust him? I knew how his mood could change like the weather?

'Listen to me. It began with an expedition. I was going in the car with him, a visit to the coffee house, and then to see one of the factories he managed. It will be a lesson, a first, a second and a third lesson, but before that there will be nourishment for a young boy, to make him big and strong, like his father. That's what he said as he stood looking at his face in the mirror, smoothing his hair. Don't you think I'm rather handsome, Gregor. Would you like to grow up to look like me?

'I had a glass of milk and cake in the café. Father drank wine, and people came to speak to him. I listened, but didn't understand. I thought, maybe Angelia will come, and every time the door opened, I hoped she would walk through. But she never came.

'We went on to a factory and I was greatly excited knowing I'd see at last the place he worked. I imagined it would be grand like the great villa.'

Gregor turned away from the drawing.

'I can't face him anymore. Listen to me, my friends. I can't look at my father.'

'Then stop, now,' Ruby said.

'I never knew what his work was,' Gregor continued, ignoring her. 'He never dirtied his fine white hands. It appeared he was important enough to be connected with the great Steel Barons themselves, and to speak with der Führer on the telephone before breakfast, or so he always told me. What did they talk about? Maybe not a word he told me was true. If it were true, what was he doing taking me in through those great doors into a vast dark hall gleaming with machinery? Oh, that place, it was Hell—the intense heat of the forge, the hammering and screeching of machines.

'I stalled at the entrance but he pushed me forward. I covered my ears. His fingers dug into my shoulder and we walked into the darkness.

'I saw the men, slaves of the Reich, the inferior race. They were lined up for inspection. Their striped shirts hung from angular shoulders. I didn't know it was possible to be so thin. They held their caps in their hands. Their eyes down at the floor, their heads shaved and branded with the letter P. P for Poland. P for Poland, I tell you.

'My father examined them as they stood to attention. He prodded one man in the ribs with a stick. Then he turned and said, your first lesson, my son. He walked away and left me.

'I couldn't move. He seemed to be gone an age. One man looked up and stared at me. And I stared back. His face was like the picture of a skull I had in my book of fairy tales, his eyes dark and hollow and his lips stretched thin across his jaw. I wanted to give something. I put my hand in my pocket and found an acorn, and I stepped forward. He rocked a little, steadied himself by clutching the man next to him. He reached forward. I saw my father was returning. The man staggered and fell.

'This is the end of the first lesson, my father said. Have you stood your ground? He kicked the man carelessly in the ribs, before gripping my arm and turning me away. These people are the foundation of everything Germany is building. They will be honoured for that. If they die in the process, this is of no importance. This must be understood, and sentimentality must never cloud your thinking.

'Sometimes, even now, I see them. Their hands are outstretched towards me. I fumble in my pockets to see if I have food to give them, desperate, knowing there's so little time before I wake. But it's not like that. What happened can't be undone.

'What were the second and third lessons? He never told me. The prisoners will be long dead, but still I see them, still I search for something to give.'

He looked around at everyone.

'Have you heard me? Do you understand? I should never have told him about Johanne. And because I did, ah, that's why in the end my father killed my sister. Not with his own hands, but in a much colder way, by his lack of love. How will you now judge me, Willoughby Stone? Guilty, no doubt? Guilty.'

'Shut up, shut up, Gregor. Enough.' Ruby grabbed him, shook him. 'How long do we have to endure this? You were a little boy. You were younger than Moonlight.'

He looked at her for a moment, as if, suddenly waking, he was surprised to find she was there. He shook his head, prised her hands from his shoulders.

'I hold food out to you too, all of you. I search the market, I make food and you eat, but it never gets any better. Nothing ever gets better. You take, and you take and it's never enough. It's over. I need to go.'

'Then go,' Ruby shouted. 'I hate you, I hate you.' She gave one cry, and turned away.

They heard his footsteps on the landing, and the door of his room close. Willoughby went to the easel and unpinned the drawing, turned it face down on the table.

Moonlight was the first to speak, in a frightened voice.

'How did you know what his father looked like if he's dead now and you never met him?'

'I didn't.'

'But you must have known something.'

'I tried to draw Gregor. Maybe it's just that he looks like his father.'

She shook her head.

'That's not what he said.'

She left, went to her room, lay on her bed, and listened for Gregor. She hoped his door would open, and she could run out to help him. But in the end everything happened too quickly, and she only sprang up in time to see him rushing down the stairs. The front door banged behind him, and he was gone. She collapsed onto her stomach and sobbed into the pillow.

Ruby went to the window as Gregor walked swiftly down the street. He wore his long winter coat, and the canvas bag over his shoulder bulged full. He's going to her, to Leda Godwin. Her rage fell away, and she sat, weak and trembling, on the bed.

In her room, Birdy sat on the chair, hands folded, head bowed. She moaned as she rocked.

Monica went down to the kitchen and made milky coffee in a jug, her expressionless face betraying nothing of her dismay. Philadelphia followed her, lit a cigarette and sat at the table.

'That was bad,' she said.

Monica said nothing, but poured coffee for her and put it on the table. There were biscuits somewhere too. In the top cupboard? She'd squirrelled them away for another day. For tonight.

After a while SA Pete looked in.

'You should go to your little girl,' he said to Philadelphia. 'She's in a bit of a state.'

Philadelphia got up in a daze and left the kitchen. SA Pete sat down heavily at the table, listening for the sound of the door.

'He was our rock,' he said to Monica. Monica didn't respond. She dunked her biscuit into the coffee, and pushed the packet to SA Pete. 'Our rock,' he said again, as if to himself, and took a biscuit.

Ruby watched Willoughby unpinning the drawings from the wall. Her head pounded.

'And now what? I brought all that nice food for us. It seems like an age ago—probably less than an hour—what with all the drama.' She flopped back on the bed and pulled the blankets round her. 'Port, Stilton cheese and cream crackers, baklava. I don't feel like any of it except the port.'

'Ruby.' Willoughby knelt beside her.

'Don't touch me. It's too much. Come downstairs with me, I don't want to stay here.'

Moonlight curled tight next to Philadelphia. She hadn't shared her mother's bed for a long time. She would like to tell her about the gun in SA Pete's room, and the terrible fear she had that Gregor would steal it. But it would only make everything even worse. In her mind she saw Gregor sitting on the parapet of the bridge at night, holding the revolver to his head. He would pull the trigger. He would fall, down into the black water. Nobody would ever find him before his body fell apart as food for the eels.

Philadelphia's arms were round her. It should have been tranquil and sweet, lying beside her mother, but something awful usually precipitated these precious moments. Her mother was lost in melancholy, and as fragile as she'd ever been. Her mother was like an empty shell.

SA Pete sat at his open window, the dog curled asleep on the floor beside him. He gave one agonised shout to a God who, in that moment, seemed to have abandoned everyone. He knew his own sins were far greater than Gregor von

Loeben's. He had maimed a man, had blackmailed and killed another before Jesus had redeemed him. Yet Gregor von Loeben, having committed no crime, suffered like the damned for being the innocent son of a Nazi.

No God answered his cry, only the wind in the tree, a distant police siren, someone's high heels striking the pavement. Only the echo of loneliness came back to him. If only there was someone, a woman, living flesh and blood, not this abstract God, who in a moment had abandoned everyone to the evil of Gregor's father. But what am I, he thought? Evil. A brute. Look at my face. I've killed people. I'm an ugly bastard. What woman would want anything to do with me?

He thought of Philadelphia, and knew it was she who had saved him from shooting himself. It was Philadelphia who had taken away his revolver, and left the note. Philadelphia, grieving and abandoned, was the miracle. He resolved he would be kind to her. Tomorrow he'd buy white roses and leave them by her door. He knelt on the floor, next to the dog, put his arms round her and sniffed her warm-dog smell.

Ruby moved her hands slowly to the music that still played on the radio. Shadows of her fingers, like strange underwater creatures, fell over the walls. Willoughby wanted to touch her, but she was lost to him. He cleared away the empty bottle of port and glasses, blew out the candles and went up to his own room.

He didn't sleep. The drawings were gathered in a pile on the table. He made tea and then sat at his table and turned each drawing up to scrutinise it. Had he really drawn Gregor's father, or was that only Gregor's perception? Gregor hadn't seen his father, after all, not even a photograph of him, since childhood. Where did ideas, visions come from? Best not to look too deeply into the unknown. It would be too easy to get lost. It could make one blind.

The door opened and Ruby peered in.

'Willoughby, are you awake? I can't sleep. You shouldn't have left me.'

'I can't sleep either.'

She came in and knelt beside him.

'I was thinking, if Gregor does come back, maybe we should leave this house. Go away somewhere peaceful. Somewhere quiet in the mountains, or by the sea, away from the city. Or even leave London and go back to Holland.'

He said nothing.

She reached her hand up, touched the back of his neck.

'What is it?' she asked, feeling him tense.

'But it wouldn't change anything, would it?' he said. 'Where in the world can you go when all the trouble is in your own head? You just take it with you. I know, believe me.'

'It would mean he got away from everything here. From constantly facing people he thinks hate him for being German.'

He was silent for a moment, then burst out. 'Don't leave. Please don't leave.'

The urgency in his voice surprised her.

'Willo?' She sat on his knee, and turned his face to hers.

'Oh.' She hadn't realised—that ardent light in his dark eyes. How stupid she was not to have realised. 'Don't look at me like that.'

She kissed her fingers and put them gently over his eyes.

'I'm not worthy of your love,' she said. 'I really don't deserve you at all.'

Gregor walked. There was peace now, moving through the night, along quiet roads; restful to look up at the lighted rooms where strangers slept and dreamed, or lay together. The residents of Gladstone Terrace, how they dragged at him, wanting and watching, until he found no rest in any corner of the house. There was a kind of peace in the continual motion of his feet. He would become nocturnal. The darkness gave him comfort. He walked through the night.

As morning drew nearer he booked into a hotel on the edge of a park. He thought he'd wandered a long way from the warehouse and Leda, but discovered he'd walked in circles, and the hotel was no distance away from her. He was shown to a small room in the top of the Georgian building—white walls, white bed cover, a bunch of bronze chrysanthemums in a glass jug on the desk.

He took Willoughby's drawing of his father from his coat, unfolded it, and gazed at that face.

If you came to me now would you be repentant? Could you bear even to look at your life?

The voice replied—*I only did my best. I did what I was asked to do. I would do it all again.*

The face no longer seemed familiar—as he stared it seemed to scatter into fragments in front of his eyes, so he saw only pencil marks on the paper. He took a match and struck it. He gazed into the flame and let it burn down to his fingers. He couldn't, in the end, set fire to the portrait. *My father.* He shivered, uncontrollably, wrapped the blankets round him, and stretched out on the bed.

When he woke, it was afternoon. The sun streamed a diagonal beam across the carpet. He got up, paid his bill and walked out of the hotel to the park. Time no longer made sense. Leaving Gladstone Terrace seemed long ago. Was today Sunday, or a holiday? Had he stayed long in the hotel? He had no idea how many days he'd paid for.

It was warm for autumn. He stood under the trees and watched a group of little boys laughing and shouting as they ran across the grass, in and out of a fountain that cast a rainbow spray in the sunlight. He saw fathers playing ball, chasing and lifting and swinging their children in the air. Everywhere he looked he saw evidence of fatherly love. How different life could have been. He tried to imagine Ernst von Loeben, stiff and cold in his uniform, playing with him in the park. He tried to imagine love in his father's eyes. He couldn't. Certainly there had been moments of sweetness that had never failed to beguile Gregor, but always the abrupt change to indifference, coldness, or rage. Then, that last time, in the grandmother's house—I failed you, he'd said. I've been a terrible father.

The small boys in their wellington boots dug sticks into the earth. Older children pushed the roundabout, leaping on and off as it spun. A small hairy dog bounded up to Gregor. He crouched down to stroke it. A woman shouted, Bertie come, and it rushed off.

He felt coldness in his heart, as if, for a moment, all sensibility had frozen. He stopped under the shade of the trees, dropped to his knees and leant against the ribbed trunk. The dry leaves floated down. He plucked a few stems of grass, twisted them and tied them into a knot, laid it down, and then another. He placed his twists of grass in a row. Then he looked up at the sky. The leaves moved in the slight breeze, and the voices of children seemed distant.

My father was a terrible man—he tormented the prisoners, he was cold to my mother, and cruel to Mari-Louise. And yet I loved him with all my puny strength. I loved him. I love him still.

After Willoughby left for work early in the morning, Ruby went back to her own room. She dressed and took the revolver from its covering of silk in her drawer. Was it loaded? What would it feel like to pull the trigger –to kill? Certainly SA Pete could tell her. Perhaps her father could have done so too. He could have told her how he'd fought for liberation from the Nazis. Peace was so hard won. Always.

As she knelt on the floor, the revolver in her lap, she remembered being pushed in her perambulator along the path through the forest. The leaves had danced in the sunlight, and beyond the leaves was the blue sky. Her mother's face had looked down at her—those eyes, smudged with sadness. She'd seen grief long before she had a name for it. It had cast a long shadow over everything—it was there in her grandparents and aunts, in the music they played, the way they spoke. Her mother would sit on a rug in the woods and draw, just as Willoughby did now, with silent concentration. And Ruby, who was then Dora, would hold a crayon in her tiny hands and stab her frustration into holes in the paper.

One day she found her mother sitting alone, staring through the window, one hand on her cheek, so still it seemed she was turned to stone. 'Be happy, Mama,' she commanded.

Her mother had smiled, her face lit up. Her smile was so rare. 'I'm not sad all the time. How can I be sad when I have you, my little girl?'

'You're sad because Papa isn't here. Where is my Papa?'

Her mother had drawn her close. She spoke so quietly, hesitantly, that Ruby had to keep reminding her to continue her story. 'Your Papa was brave. He was in what we called the Resistance. It was very dangerous, and I was always frightened for him, for both of us. One night the Gestapo burst into the flat where we lived in Amsterdam, and took us to prison. I never saw your papa, my Kai, again.'

Alone in her bed, Ruby had sobbed for her father.

My father was taken to the beach. That was where they took their prisoners—the ones who had betrayed Germany. He was younger than I am now. I'm not a good person, no hero. But I love Gregor and maybe I would die for him, if it came to it. Pray for me, she whispered, thinking of SA Pete. I feel madness in my head, like thousands of wasps buzzing.

Ruby put the revolver in her wicker basket, put on her shoes and coat and left the house. She walked down the street towards the river. Oh that I could meet Gregor coming home. But she passed only strangers, who gave her no more than a glance. She smiled, thinking, they don't know that in this ridiculous basket with its bunch of plastic flowers stitched on the side, next to my purse and gloves, is a revolver. It belonged to a man who believes an angel in the form of a woman stole it from him to prevent his suicide. An angel saved his life.

She went down narrow streets between warehouses, heard the plop of a rat, the lapping of water against the dockside. She whispered to herself, like a mad woman, rehearsing what she might say to Leda Godwin. I am walking in the wilderness. I am no longer in control. Anything might happen and I'll abandon myself to my fate. She turned into the yard and crossed the cobbles to the entrance of the warehouse. A cold heat ran up and down her spine. She shivered.

The passageways and stairs led her up to the room where the dancers rehearsed. She found herself on the edge of the empty studio, unable to see the stairs to the next floor, to Leda's makeshift apartment. Blackout blinds shut out the light, and the studio was in darkness, except for one wall where a film played. She stood, confused, in the cold light of the screen where an image played—a man in silhouette holding the hand of a little boy. Everything in the film was grey—their long coats, the broken buildings behind them, the sky. She heard the fall of their feet over the rubble, and the wild moaning of the wind. They walked until they were swallowed by complete darkness. Only the relentless sound of the wind remained.

She had arrived in the warehouse as a bizarre performance was taking place, yet there was no audience but her. It could be a dress rehearsal, but she could see no director, and nobody asked her to leave. She might as well be invisible.

A spotlight shone in the middle of the floor where a man and woman in black evening dress whirled round each other like menacing insects, a small, tight dance, never touching—uneasy, electric. They whispered a hard, guttural non-language, their heads tilted towards each other and away.

Barrel organ music broke into a tango, the room was flooded with harsh light, and a group of dancers ran into the studio wheeling a pram. The pram was spun and tipped up,

171

as they whirled round with their blank white faces. Ruby stood in their midst, unable to move.

'I'm carrying a revolver,' she said as the dancers spun past. 'It's in my bag.'

A gaunt mannish woman with a gash of red lipstick burst into laughter, and the others echoed the laughter as they danced round her.

She covered her face, overcome with weakness, as if her legs might give way. She took a deep breath. When she dared to look again she saw, with a start, Leda Godwin standing motionless the other side of the studio, watching her. Leda's face was expressionless. There was that wasp-like buzzing in Ruby's ears, and terror rushed in. She knew at last who it was Leda Godwin reminded her of—Aunt Gitta.

She was a little child again, waking in her bed as bright light was shone in her face. At first she couldn't see anything, only heard a woman whispering in German. It was Aunt Gitta—a stranger. *Du bist ein boses Mädchen.* This demonic aunt stared down, pulling at Ruby's bedclothes, shining a light in her face and whispering over and over the same words in an urgent voice. Ruby cried out in terror and revulsion. She was going to be eaten alive. Gitta clamped her hand to her face. *Halt den Mond. Du bist ein boses Mädchen.*

The dancers fell back. Leda Godwin walked across the room towards her. Ruby swayed, blanked out, collapsed. When she opened her eyes again Leda was kneeling beside her.

'You're not well.' Her voice sounded kind. 'You must go home. Don't worry about Gregor. Everything is all right. You must let go now, Ruby.'

Gregor walked swiftly by the river to the ruined church. It was early evening. People were leaving work, bent on getting home and in from the cold—fog hung in the air—the sweet sharp song of a blackbird pierced the gloom. He went through the gate into the garden of the church.

Peace fell as he wandered the paths alone, through the golden leaf-meal, into the roofless nave. The walls were cold and wet with moss. He ran his hand down the stone, down to the earth. He crouched and took the drawing of his father from his pocket.

He didn't look at the portrait again. He folded it four times, and then, with a piece of sharp stone, he scraped a narrow slit into the soil. Briefly he held the folded paper to his lips, then pressed it into the slit, pushing it down with the stone, until nothing could be seen.

He sat for a long time on one of the benches, eyes closed. The numbness in his heart and mind was a relief, but it didn't last. He shivered with damp and cold. Leda said that he should come whenever he wanted. He didn't know what he wanted—except to be in that room on the top floor—to be with Leda. He stood up stiffly, stretched, and set off for the warehouse. His steps quickened with urgency.

He went up the stairs. He heard piano music coming from the dance studio, the same phrases played over and over. As he reached the door, he saw a young dancer crouch down to start the tape recorder once more, then run across the floor to sit on a wooden chair, a bundle of grey silk at her feet. The room was dark except for one lamp in the corner.

The music started again, softly, a run of notes, chords in a minor key. Slowly she reached down, took a corner of the shawl and drew it across her arm, wrapping it round her shoulders. As she twisted from one position to another, the shawl took on a new form—it became her evening gown, her dancing partner, her lover. So powerful was the illusion she created, that it seemed she no longer danced alone. The shawl was her baby, the dead child she laid down on the ground. As the music ended she stretched out on the floor and wrapped it over her like a shroud. She lay still for a moment, then she sprang up and ran across the studio to wind back the music. With her shawl, she practised the opening moves, glancing in the mirror to check her positions.

How beautiful it was. He wanted to tell her. Would his words be an intrusion? He hesitated, and she caught sight of his image in the mirror. He went in and closed the door behind him. He'd never seen her before, but she reached out her hand to him. The music played. They began to dance, weaving round each other, without touching more than the tips of their fingers. Gregor remembered how to hold, how to let his partner lean into him, to lift her, as if effortlessly, from the floor. She no longer seemed separate from him; it was as if, divested of all thoughts, they were one body, lost in the glorious, overwhelming flow of movement.

The music stopped. They held hands for a moment and smiled, their eyes full of light, but spoke no words. Gregor left the room as quietly as he'd entered. She picked up her shawl and went back to the tape recorder.

He went up to Leda's floor, but she wasn't there. He felt changed by the dance. He thought, maybe it doesn't matter who or what we love. Love is sufficient unto itself. I love my sister with all my heart. I love my father.

Leda Godwin seemed like a miracle to him; that she had been standing watching him the night the birds had circled the sky over the river; had watched him busking with Ruby so many times; that she had sought and found him. He sat at the table and turned to the windowsill. The feather had gone. So she had moved it in her sleep after all, he thought. He laughed in a moment of disbelief, of startling joy at the marvel of such an inconsequential miracle.

Ruby staggered, exhausted, out of a taxi. Willoughby, seeing her from the end of the street as he walked back from work, rushed to help her up the steps and into the house.

'I'm so weak. What's wrong with me?'

'You're very hot. You've got a fever.'

He helped her up to her room and into bed. He left to get her water, and when he returned, her eyes were glassy-bright, her face damp and flushed.

'Where's my basket? Did I leave it in the cab?'

'It's on the floor with your coat.'

He fetched it for her. She grabbed it from him and rummaged inside.

'Strange. That's very strange.'

'What's strange, Ruby?'

'Nothing. Maybe it's not important.'

She thought, SA Pete's revolver was in my basket when I went out. It's gone. I could be arrested for having it illegally. For a moment she was gripped by panic, then she sighed. Do I care anyway? She tried to tell Willoughby what had happened.

'I feel as if I'm in a dream and I can't wake up. I don't know anything. I went to the warehouse to find Gregor. What a bizarre place. On the first floor someone was screening a film on the wall, an image of a man walking slowly through a ruined city. It was so sad, Willoughby, and I couldn't stop watching it. I don't know why.' Her eyes filled with tears. She wiped them away with the corner of her silk bedspread. 'And this grotesque couple dancing round each other and whispering gibberish, Then, out of nowhere, a gang of people in blank white masks rushed on with a baby in a pram, and I couldn't escape. They kept whirling round, pushing and shouting, and I was trapped in the middle.

'I knew someone was watching me. I saw Leda Godwin the other side of the room, completely still, staring at me. I mistook her for my Aunt Gitta. The next thing I knew I was on the floor. She was kneeling beside me.'

Willoughby stroked the hair away from her face—Ruby had never seemed so vulnerable before.

'I suppose it was just some kind of rehearsal I got tangled up in. I should know, being my mother's child. I went to all sorts of rehearsals when I was little. But it seemed real. I

175

only went to find Leda Godwin. I wanted to see if she knew where Gregor had gone. I think that's why I went. Though I might have intended to kill her. Perhaps that was it. If those dancers hadn't unsettled me I might have shot her.'

'Ruby, what the hell are you talking about?'

'Nothing. Everything. Shooting her. I had a revolver in my bag, but it's gone now. Something else happened, Aunt Gitta appeared, like a ghoul, and I fainted. Leda Godwin put me in the cab, sent me home.' She cried quietly. 'Don't leave me.'

He sat beside her mattress so he could manoeuvre his arm round her.

When she drifted in to sleep, he tried to shift—the weight of her head was heavy on his chest, and her face so hot, he needed to take away the blanket.

'Don't go,' she said, clutching his hand.

Leda expressed no surprise to see Gregor sitting at the table when she returned.

'I thought you might be here.'

'I had to come,' he said, getting to his feet.

She took off her green coat, draped it over the back of her chair.

'Were you here long?'

'I'm not sure. An hour maybe?'

'You missed Ruby. She came looking for you, or me. She walked into the middle of a rehearsal.'

'Ruby came? Didn't she stay?'

'I got a cab for her. She wasn't well.'

He brushed his hands over his eyes. It was impossible to think about Ruby. 'I left the house some days ago. I seem to have lost track of time somehow.'

'Ah, yes. So it seems.'

She stood with her back to the window, her face in shadow, and picked up one of the stones, turning it slowly, as if studying its patterns. She appeared to wait for him to speak.

'Have I told you everything?' he asked. It seemed imperative that nothing should be lost.

'Have you? Only you know that.' She put the stone down and looked up at him.

'I told you everything I remember. Is it enough? For your writing—is there anything else?'

'There's more than enough—for the rest of my life, Gregor.' She stepped into the light, gave that brief smile that had become familiar to him. 'There's something I can tell you,' she began.

He thought—she has tears in her eyes. She sighed deeply.

'The children's nursery—I have a clear vision of you and your sister running through the woods to find it. It haunts me, as if I know the place. Like a half-remembered dream.

'Last night I remembered that I read about it many years ago. I read such a lot about Germany when I was very young—driven to make sense of it all, to try to understand.' She spoke quickly in a low voice. 'Do you want to know? I'll tell you all I can. I don't have the sources any longer, but I couldn't sleep, and it came back to me in those long hours before dawn.

'There were prisoners of war. They were made to work, unpaid of course, in the munitions factories all over Germany—for the war effort. Men and women, and even children. At first, if they were married, they were permitted to share barracks, and so the women fell pregnant, and their babies were born. What to do but build a concentration camp for infants. Of course, naturally! Only the depraved could dream such a thing.

'The mothers, to begin with, were allowed to visit on Sundays. Then it stopped—the women were needed for more work. No time for days off. Nobody cared. They were only the nameless babies of Jews and Poles and Slavs, after all. Why should they care? There were other concerns. The allies were gaining control. Germany was lost.

'I read all this when I was eleven years old. Not one child survived. They starved, or died of dysentery. I understood then our capacity for evil, how commonplace and ordinary it is, how easily decent simple people can fall.' She put her hand over her heart. 'My life was changed from that moment. All innocence had gone.

'And now…only this is important—out of the horror of that camp, you brought me your beautiful sister, and Johanne Kuhn—you gave me your child's heart, struggling to survive and make sense of it. As I did then. As I still do. It is enough Gregor. It's more than enough.'

'I know,' he said. 'I understand.' There was something, new and unfamiliar, impossible to explain. Like looking through coloured glass, a radiant light that transformed everything, as if, for a moment, Leda had brought Mari-Louise back.

'I didn't tell you the most important thing.' He gazed beyond Leda, to the deep blue darkening sky through the window. 'I loved my father.' The words caught in his throat. 'Wherever he is—and he must surely be dead—despite everything, I love him still.'

'How could you not? You're bonded. You're his son. It's natural.'

'And in desperation for his love in return, I betrayed my sister.'

'No Gregor,' she said, emphatically. 'Your love never made you culpable for his crimes. You were a child. You longed to please him. There was no betrayal. You must not believe that any longer.' She touched his hand. 'It's as simple as that.'

Everything he was going to say fell away—a sense of calm had fallen over the room.

I was on my way here, he thought, and I saw the young dancer. It was a most beautiful thing. I realise now she danced for Mari-Louise. Or was it more than that? It was if she became my sister as she danced, my beloved sister holding the dead baby, my sister, the love and despair in her eyes?

Leda gave him a look as if she was about to say something, and then didn't. For a moment they stood listening to the music from the studio below.

'And the feather, it's gone.' He glanced at the sill, remembering. 'Did you move it?'

'Of course.'

He met her eyes.

'A miracle?'

She smiled in answer, and continued to look at him. Sometimes, when he was little, his sister had looked at him in that way, a look of curiosity and love, as if she gazed beyond his face into his heart.

'I'm going away,' she said at last.

He felt the shock, like blow.

'Where? Where are you going?'

'I was going to find you, to ask you to come here one last time,' she continued, softly. 'But here you are anyway. I'm going back home. I was only ever here for a year at the most. I've done all the work I can for now. It needs time to ferment before I return and complete it.'

'I hadn't expected...' His mind crowded with things he wanted to say, but they stuck in his throat.

She went to the bookshelf and reached for a cardboard box.

'In here are the tapes we've made, or to be accurate, the tapes you made.' She put them down on the desk. 'I've transposed them all, word for word, and my notes will go with me until I find a way to use them. Your voice—I'll never forget that. Nor the hours we spent in this room. Do you want the tapes?'

'I don't know.'

'We can destroy them, or they can be deposited somewhere, anywhere. Buried?' Again that brief smile—

this time of gentle amusement. 'Though burial is an eccentric thing to do to a box of cassettes.'

'I don't know yet.'

'And now…you must go back to your people, to Moonlight and Ruby. To the others.' She poured brandy into the blue-rimmed glasses, and passed one to him. 'Thank you,' she said, and raised her glass. 'Thank you, Gregor von Loeben, for your extraordinary story.'

Willoughby cycled quickly back from work, dashed into the house, and straight up to see Ruby. She was sitting up in bed, seemed fully recovered after a long sleep, and was rummaging through her capacious bag.

'Not the money,' she said. 'There's hardly any of that, so nobody would bother.' She drew a battered green leather wallet out, and searched the pockets.

'Thank goodness. It's still there! It hasn't gone, like the other thing.'

'What?'

'The photograph of my parents. I had a dream it'd gone, along with the other thing that disappeared when I collapsed on Leda Godwin's warehouse floor.' She took a photograph from the pocket. 'I couldn't bear to lose it.'

She passed it to Willoughby. He saw a man and woman standing under a tree. The man was young, graceful, and startlingly attractive, with the same dark eyes and wild curly hair as Ruby. The woman, small, dark-haired, with an intense gaze, looked older by at least ten years.

'My parents—Hedda Brandt and Kai Hoffman—my mother was German, as you know. My father was half Dutch, half Spanish. But I've told you that before. It was taken in 1942 in Amsterdam.'

Willoughby looked long at the photograph.

'They look so happy,' he said.

'They were still in love. No time for the bloom to fade, no time even to get married. They were arrested nine months later. In June 1943, when Mama was still in prison, my father was taken and shot by the Gestapo.'

'Christ, Ruby.' Willoughby gazed down at the photograph unable to say more.

'I am the miracle child. I rose from the ashes of Nazi Netherlands. Don't look like that, Willo. I've lived with it all a long time. Don't cry. I'm all right. It was cathartic to have a fever. I recommend it, especially with you to look after me. And now, I'm here. We're both here.' Sadness cast a shadow over her face. She picked at a thread of silk on her dressing gown. 'For a long time I thought Gregor and I would be free one day from the ghosts of our fathers – Gregor's Nazi, and my equally weighty Hero of the Dutch Resistance. I know now that it's for probably for life, Gregor's guilt, my...' She fell silent.

'Your what?'

'*Du bist ein boses Mädchen,*' Ruby whispered. 'That's what Aunt Gitta told me.'

'Translate.'

'I've told you before. It means, you're an evil girl. Don't look so shocked. I know I'm not that bad. But I fall a long way short of my extraordinary and heroic parents. Aunt Gitta put her hand over my mouth to stop me crying that night. It was awful. But that's enough. I'm exhausted and don't want to talk about it anymore. The end. What about your father Willoughby? I don't know a thing about your family.'

'Mine? Oh, he was a good sort. We lived together, my father, grandmother and me,' he said quietly. 'My mother died soon after I was born, and Dad took me back to his mother. My grandmother brought me up.'

'Ah, it makes sense to me. I can see why.'

'Why what?'

'Why you're as you are,' she replied.

He smiled.

'It's like you to be so frustratingly oblique, just at the point when I thought you'd noticed me.'

'Oh, I notice you, believe me. Is your dad still alive?'

He shook his head.

'Died. Lung cancer. Too much smoking.'

'That's sad, Willo.'

She closed her eyes, sleepy, thoughts drifting. Willoughby loved her, of course. She knew that. Why else would he be so kind? She took his hand. And what has happened to that damned revolver? I hope it doesn't land me in trouble. How wonderful that Gregor walked on the river in my dream, with the sunlight behind him, like Christ.

'I have always thought there was something Christ-like about Gregor,' she said, opening her eyes. 'It's so tiresome to be surrounded by good people.'

She hummed quietly, a hymn.

'What was the other thing?' he asked.

'What do you mean?'

'When you looked in your bag you said, thank goodness that's not gone too.'

She lifted his hand, turned it over and kissed his palm.

'Nothing of consequence. It was only a revolver. Even your hand smells of pencils.'

Leda and Gregor walked together, out through the courtyard into the autumn night. Leda carried two plastic bags of books. She stopped at a bus stop.

'I must leave you here,' she said.

'I'll wait with you.'

When the bus arrived, he followed her on. She gave a sidelong look of surprise, but didn't demur. They climbed to the top and sat at the front. A light rain fell, like mist in the orange glow of the streetlights. She shivered. He took her hand and gazed from the window as the bus journeyed alongside the river and over a bridge—he had no idea where. Derelict places, late-night shops, corners where dogs picked over the debris. Something stopped him asking where she was going and why. Her hand lay unmoving under his.

The bus drew into a bleak interchange. She stood up to get off and he went with her.

'I must go now, Gregor.' She turned to face him, and drew her coat round her. 'I'm so tired.'

'Don't go yet,' he begged. 'It's too sudden, too soon, much too soon.'

She hesitated a moment, seemed torn, and then walked towards the coffee bar.

'We can stop here for a while. Will that be enough?'

There were few people—two men reading newspapers, and an old woman half-dozing, her hands clasped round her teacup. The wall was covered with sepia photographs of cows and sheep. Spider plants trailed down over the patches of condensation.

Leda brought coffee, brushed away a scattering of crumbs and put the mugs down on the table. It seemed a desperate place to say goodbye. He wanted to say so much to her before it was too late, but he felt so unpractised in professing love. Not since his boyhood fantasy of Angelia had he loved a woman. He was overcome by the immensity of his feeling and the inadequacy of words.

'You know nothing about me, Gregor.' She looked at him with her clear grey eyes, as if she knew what it was he struggled to express. 'Can you really love what you don't know?'

'I do know you.' But when he tried to attach some quality to her, she seemed to slip away. He lowered his eyes.

'Who are you? You've never let me know anything.'

'I told you I write plays. I've written biography. You can find out all about my work if you choose. But that's not what you mean, is it? The truth is, my own life feels of little significance. I'm not interested in myself. It's so easy to step into the lives of others. Sometimes it seems I could let go of the will to live, drift away and never wake up. But other lives have a hold on me. Those stories. Other people keep me here, pinned to the world.'

He reached for her hands again. Gently she disengaged them, shook her head.

'Oh, I know it sounds unlikely, but it's true enough. I owe you so much more than I can ever give, Gregor.' She looked down at the table, at his hands, and briefly rested hers over them. 'But there's one thing I can tell you before we say goodbye.

'I came to London last October, just over a year ago—for research, or maybe *to search* is more accurate. I encountered you the first day. You and Ruby were busking one afternoon at World's End. After that I often saw you. I began to search you out deliberately. One day in January—a bright day, but changeable, the skies suddenly darkened and snow fell—you both appeared out of the snowstorm, as if scarcely touched by the cold. Ruby played, in that abandoned way she has, and as you danced, I felt a soaring in my mind, as if for a moment everything opened up and light streamed in. As graphic as that—the dismal streets were changed—a transcendent moment.' She smiled and looked directly into Gregor's eyes. 'There aren't many of those in a lifetime, are there? There was a quality of otherness about you both that drew me, and for a week or two I saw you every day. She has a great gift for music—your gift is exceptional in another way—impossible to describe. When I met you in Antonio's I knew in a moment it was you I wanted to talk to. Ruby has too much resistance. She creates great commotion and illusion. She seems to be generous and open, but she guards her heart very carefully, it seems to me.'

She looked down at the table, absently moved the teaspoon.

'You only talk of Ruby and me, Leda. Tell me something about you.'

'Me? I'm nobody special. What can I tell you? I've made an odd kind of career. I love the colour green.'

'I know that!'

'I loved my father. When he was called up to fight in the war, I stood at the window long after he'd gone. I know about silence, the unspoken traumas. The secrets people take with them when they die. You need know nothing else about me. There's always too much talk where there should be silence. And, from time to time, too much silence where there should be talk. And that's all. I'm tired. I need to go now.'

She got up, put on her coat. For a moment Gregor watched her as if in a dream. Then, as the door of the café closed, he grabbed his coat and dashed out. A bus drew up, and for a moment he lost sight of her. When he caught up with her, she looked cornered.

'Let me go now. We're much too far out already.'

'What do you mean?'

She embraced him, then stood back, her hands lightly touching his head.

'I'll arrange for someone to send the tapes. Goodbye Gregor.'

He stood, rooted to the spot as she walked out of sight.

'The German master, is he back yet?' Monica asked Philadelphia when she encountered her peering into kitchen cupboards.

Philadelphia shrugged. 'Will he ever come back?'

Monica's face clouded. She played with a fake gold chain dangling round her neck that Gregor had once given her.

'I don't like to think he won't. Where would I go? With Birdy?'

Philadelphia didn't answer. She was thinking of the first night she'd stayed at the house, how Gregor had listened to her when she sat crying at the table. It was the same table she sat at now, lifting the saltcellar and making a trail of salt, but it was bleak without him. He'd made a chicken casserole that night, in a round brown pot with a lid, and they'd had it with bread. She'd never tasted anything so good, nor felt so content. You can stay here, he'd said. She only had to look at that brown pot on the shelf. It made her sad now, in his absence. She would ask him to teach her to cook when, if, he came back.

Now Gregor was away, SA Pete had stepped in, surprising her, with flowers, and chocolate, and, like Gregor, never touching her—always respectful. It was unfortunate she wasn't romantically interested in either of them—life remained utterly unsatisfactory.

Birdy, her long white plait draped over her shoulder, stooped over her knitting. She listened for the sound of the front door, and the quiet footfall she knew so well on the stairs. When she left her room to go to the bathroom, she found Moonlight in a handstand against the wall. The child turned upright again.

'Why doesn't he come back? Will he ever come back?' Moonlight said, her voice trembling with fear.

Birdy touched her cheek, and smiled. She tried to say that all would be well. They must just wait. But the words stuck, as they always did, and only her strange little cries sounded. The child put her arms round her, and they stood, locked together.

Willoughby, fearing the worst, went up to Gregor's room. He felt the weight of responsibility. Gregor's outburst had been unforeseen and bewildering for them all. There must have been something he should have done to calm him down. He opened the door carefully, feeling as if he was intruding.

The room looked as if nobody lived in it. The mattress was covered with a white cloth. There were no clothes, no possessions except the paperback books in their neat stacks. It looked as if Gregor might have planned his departure and packed before that night.

He turned to the window—on the sill was a white candle in an oak holder, and a page of notepaper.

Willoughby read his name, and the words that followed.

Dear friend. The faces you draw have their own life. You have no idea of their power. It would be less dangerous if you understood this.

The number 47 will take you back, Leda had said.

'You've neglected to look after yourself for too long. You care for everyone else instead. You must rest now, go home.' There had been kindness in her eyes. She held his gaze, and he couldn't look away. *'Self-love, my liege, is not so vile a sin as self-neglecting,'* she said softly. 'Goodbye, Gregor.'

She'd walked away without looking back. He stood, unmoving, longing for her to turn. But she disappeared up the ramp and around the corner into the street.

I should have thanked her, he realised, and, mortified at his failure, he started to run after her. But he checked himself. Already it felt too late. It would be awkward and unwanted—she would be distant. I should have thanked her on the bus. Why else did I come to this desolate place?

He went back to the café, where, only a moment before, they'd sat opposite each other, hands clutched round their coffee. The door was locked. Inside, an old woman in a green overall lifted chairs onto tables and swept underneath. He looked around—cigarette butts and litter scattered round his feet, a few desultory people, hunched into coats and scarves, waited for buses. There was the nauseating smell of rubber tyres and exhaust fumes. He felt ill-clad, damp and chilled to the bone.

There was a night bus travelling out of the city. On impulse he clambered onto it. He counted the few people— three young men, two youngsters wrapped around each other, and an old woman with a tiny dog, its nose and ears emerging from the bag on her lap. In other circumstances he might have spoken to her. But he settled into the back corner of the bus. He hoped it would be a long journey and that he could return on another bus, that it might use up some of the hours before the tube started again, and he could travel underground until daybreak. Morning came so late these October days.

He paid the conductor and arranged his scarf into a makeshift pillow against the window. The engine of the bus vibrated in his skull. He shut his eyes and drifted into a trance-like sleep, only half conscious of the stop and start of the vehicle, the atmosphere of chill that clung to people's coats as they climbed onto the bus and moved down the aisle. Sometimes he opened his eyes briefly to look. But the darkness was easier. There might be others around him in the same state, travelling out of the city and back again, through endless night.

The darkest hours passed in this place of nothing, no thoughts of past, present or future, except to get on another bus and then the tube, to try to sleep. Sometime in the night, travelling back into the city, he saw the light of the tube station. He stumbled off the bus, half asleep, down the escalator. The ill-lit platform was almost deserted—only the strange slow motion of a stationmaster walking towards him, carrying a lamp—the lamplight curiously green. Ponderously, as if waking from sleep, a tube train emerged like a monster from the tunnel. The doors swished open, and Gregor got on. The doors closed, but the train went nowhere.

It was warmer underground than on the bus. He slipped his scarf round his face and closed his eyes. He could be anywhere. He could be in some subterranean dugout, lit by greenish lamps. He thought of Leda, quiet and beautiful— she was beautiful, wasn't she, luminous—standing on the bridge, the birds whirling in their miraculous clouds overhead. He thought of Mari-Louise sitting on the floor of the children's camp. There seemed to be some connection between Mari-Louise and the dancer with the shawl. With a jolt, he realised it was Leda's work he'd seen—dance, no words—she had said she had written nothing. He thought, how extraordinary, I saw and didn't realise. I can go back, find out. The thought amazed and consoled him.

The train slid into motion at last. It filled with people as it drew nearer to the centre of the city.

'Are you all right, sir?'

Gregor pulled down his scarf and opened his eyes. A boy was staring at him.

'Yes, I'm all right.'

He felt desperate to get off the train. He reached out for the support rails, accidentally knocking a book from his neighbour's hands in his haste.

'I apologise,' he said, bending to retrieve the book.

He staggered to the door, and as the tube glided to a halt, he stepped out onto the platform, ran up the escalators and out into the pale fog of an autumn morning.

It helped to see the window upside down, though Moonlight couldn't explain why, so she spent hours doing her handstands against the landing wall outside her bedroom. When her hands and arms ached too much to do any more, she stood by the window of her little room and watched the cars go by, the faces of passengers peering out. Sometimes they seemed to look up, as if they knew her.

She'd discovered the revolver was missing from SA Pete's room. When he was out she searched everywhere she could think of, taking care, when she fumbled through drawers, to leave no sign of disturbance. She'd even looked in his bed, which was horribly crumpled and grubby. Afterwards she'd gone to Gregor's room and found nothing out of place, and no revolver, which meant only one thing— that he'd taken it with him after stealing it from SA Pete. She watched SA Pete carefully for clues. But he didn't seem disturbed in any way by the theft, and she could hardly ask him. On the contrary, he seemed more content than usual, and was unusually attentive to Philadelphia.

All this worried her intensely. The middle of the night was the hardest time. Although she was exhausted and fretful, Moonlight jolted awake every time sleep overcame her. Gregor had been gone so long. Usually he was only away a few hours.

The terror came—a vision of him floating on the water with a bullet wound in his head, his eyes open but unseeing—floating like the goldfish she'd brought home from the pet shop had floated when it died too soon. She sprang up and put on the light. It was only quarter past three. At that moment she knew there was someone at the end of her bed looking down at her. She felt the presence before she turned round.

The man was wearing a Nazi uniform. He stood at the end of her bed and gazed at her. He held a bunch of white roses. She knew there were twelve—one for every month of the year. She knew he was Gregor's father. She wasn't afraid because, unlike Gregor, he wasn't alive, so nothing could harm him.

'You must go away now,' she told him, firmly as if speaking to a child. 'This isn't your house. Go home now.' She rearranged her pillows and pulled the blankets over her eyes so she couldn't see him any longer.

She got up as soon as it was light, hid her school satchel and uniform under her bed in case anyone thought to look in her room, and pulled on her jeans and two jumpers. Free of the long night, she rushed down the stairs and out into the cold. She was certain she'd know where to go—her feet would take her. Her great love for Gregor would guide her to him. She had to find him in time—if she was too late she planned to fling herself from the bridge in the river, without further consideration. She might, if unfortunate, be saved.

A light mist hung over the river, her breath clouded in front of her and the cold rasped in her chest. She ran to the bridge, and stared down through the railings. How fast the black brown water flowed, swirling and dragging on the great stone pilings. With a jolt, she thought she saw a man in the water, swimming. She squinted, her heart hammering. Then she saw it was just a buoy. She ran down to the muddy bank by the community of houseboats.

'Did you see anyone in the water?' she asked a small scruffy boy who balanced along a plank of wood by the water.

He stared at her a moment, and wobbled off the wood into the mud. Brow furrowed, he appeared to think about it.

'I might have done.'

'Did you though? Think. It's important.'

His face lit up.

'I did actually, now I really think.' His voice was solemn, thrilled at the drama. 'I saw a man take his coat off and paddle in. Next I looked, he was up to his neck. He bobbed about and then vanished.'

'Are you sure? Absolutely.'

'Yes. When I looked again he'd vanished. Dragged under the water, I think.'

Moonlight uttered a cry and covered her face with her hands. In another moment she turned away from the boy, to pace the margin of the water, staring out until her eyes hurt.

The sun hadn't broken through the fog when Gregor ran up the steps from the underground and almost collapsed against the wall of the newsagent at the entrance to the station.

Exhausted from days without proper sleep, he took the road to the river. As he walked, the sun broke through the clouds and the sky was lit with a pearly light. How beautiful it was. There was beauty everywhere, if only he took notice.

He returned to the bridge where he'd stood, a lifetime ago it seemed, and watched the swirling flock of birds. He wondered where he would go now. He couldn't go home after the terrible night he'd found the drawings. He'd been so harsh with everyone, especially Willoughby Stone and Ruby. It seemed unlikely they'd want him back. He supposed he'd have to find a room somewhere. Thoughts crowded in. All practical considerations felt impossible. He put his hands to his head and closed his eyes. How good it would be just to slip into the water. Drowning was a comforting way to die, he'd heard, after the first panic. Slipping, floating—that sensation of leaving the body at last, leaving behind the guilt, the torment. Surrendering everything.

'Mr von Loeben.'

A child was shouting his name from the bank, someone he must know since they knew about the von. He opened his eyes, turned quickly, saw a girl, face distraught, arms waving, calling his name.

She ran up the steps as he walked towards her, and flung herself at him, sobbing inconsolably.

Moonlight knew that finding Gregor was a turning point in her life, but she couldn't find the words to describe why. Ever after, when, in the stillness of night, she thought of that extraordinary moment between them—the meaning just slipped away. Yes, she had saved his life. It was more than that though, even more than love.

She had cried, her arms round his neck, as he knelt on the pavement beside her. It was the kind of crying, impossible to stop, that came from her heart and shook her whole body.

'Everything is all right. Moonlight, everything is all right,' he kept saying.

At last her cries subsided to an occasional sob that shuddered through her rib cage. She looked at him.

'Let me see your face.'

They looked into each other's eyes for a long time. How could she explain what she saw there? Her tiny reflection— but that was only surface deep, like the skin of the river. Beneath that, the depths, something tugging her, the undertow, pulling her down into the place of everything. She shut her eyes. It was too much.

'Are you coming back now?' she asked.

'How can I?'

'What could you do instead?'

'Nothing. I have no plan.'

'Come back home then.'

He had looked into her face and she had nodded.

'It's all right, Mr Loeben. It's really all right. I made your father go. He's not in the house any longer.'

He smiled, and she took his hand. She thought—I saved his life. Her heart soared.

'Are you hungry?'

'I am.'

'Me too. Everyone will be very glad to see us.'

Hearing the front door, Birdy left her room. She knew the sound of their feet on the stairs—the child had brought him home at last. Her face lit up, and she rushed towards them, her arms outstretched. She took Gregor's hands and held them to her eyes.

It seemed to Moonlight that the old lady thought Gregor was the resurrected Christ. She looked just like a painting, Jesus with Mary in the Garden of Gethsemane.

'I saved his life,' she said.

Birdy clasped her hands together, nodding and smiling as she looked down at Moonlight.

'I'm going to make dinner,' Moonlight said, inspired. 'I won't go to school today. Maybe not at all this week, actually. What would you like to eat most of all? You can ask for anything.' She envisaged a feast, a table with golden candlesticks, cut glass bowls, bunches of grapes, cherries and pineapples.

'First I'd like to lie in the bath, and then sleep.'

'Sleep first,' she instructed. 'You will wake up a new person.'

'Gregor, you're back!' Ruby came out of her room. 'The Prodigal Cousin returns. Or should I say, the Prodigal Landlord?'

Moonlight was proud of the feast she planned for Gregor's homecoming. Monica was in charge of the kitchen, and brought the Stork Cookery book down from her room to show Moonlight the things they might prepare.

'It's going to be a party,' Moonlight said to Birdy, who sat in the corner of the kitchen smiling at them with her bright eyes. Monica mixed pastry, SA Pete polished the assorted collection of glasses and silver retrieved from the cupboard, and Moonlight mixed together chocolate, almonds and cherries.

Then there was the question of what to wear. They all examined their clothes. SA Pete had a suit he only wore for funerals, but with a floral tie in orange and red, it would pass. Monica dressed Birdy in a silver sequinned evening dress she'd had for twenty years, and herself in a navy blue twin set with a long skirt she'd bought in sale and never had the chance to wear. Philadelphia wore a green silk trouser suit with a golden belt, and wove diamonds into her hair. Oblivious of SA Pete's tender attention, she thought of the last time she'd worn diamonds in her hair, and longed for the man she'd lost to return to her. But Gregor was back. Something was restored.

Moonlight wanted to wear something stunning, but nothing she had matched her dream. If only I had some better wings, she thought. She saw herself in silver chiffon with wings attached by a sequinned harness to her back. Not the ridiculously small wings that ballet dancers had, more like the wings of the angels painted by artists. But even then, would such wings be big enough to fly with? It didn't matter. Happiness was a new feeling. She moved lightly, in the warm glow of it, and felt generous towards everyone. With her newfound confidence, she knocked on Ruby's door to ask if she had a silver dress she could borrow for the night. A little later she found a treasure of beautiful things on her bed, and sat in delight, shaking out the folds of dress after dress.

Only Willoughby, aware of the elevated atmosphere in the house, didn't enter into it. Ruby had found him in his room.

'Willo. There you are. Gregor's home, did you hear? I'm so happy.'

How beautiful it was, Moonlight thought—the sitting room transformed to a grand dining room, the table with red candles, ivy flowers from the park, the glass and silver gleaming. She had planned perfectly, and Monica had helped her cook—the chicken with gravy and roast potatoes, and three different coloured vegetables, peppers she'd never eaten before, and avocados, and pineapples. SA Pete brought boxes of Black Magic chocolate, and Philadelphia smiled.

'It's a victory,' Ruby said. 'A triumph for Moonlight, and for everyone.' She raised her glass, then they all raised glasses. They drank, except SA Pete—Birdy sipping watered-down wine, Monica robustly drinking, glass after glass.

Only Willoughby sat slightly apart. He watched them. In his imagination he drew the table with them all sitting round, their lit-up faces—laughing, listening, eating. In an instant he could see what nobody else had yet realised. He saw that SA Pete was in love with Philadelphia, but that she would never love him in return. Monica loved Birdy, though her love, close and intense, bordered on possession. Monica also loved SA Pete. He'd never know. It would never cross his mind. Monica was plain. She had never crossed anyone's mind or heart, and was resigned to living in the borders. Who did Birdy love—she was so other, she existed in another realm, lost to them all?

Moonlight, nothing like the children he encountered at the school, was fey, brittle, dreamy, and yet sharp in her observations. What would she do? Where would she go? What would happen to her?

'You're lonely,' she said, coming to stand beside him. Startled he turned to look at her as she put her hand in his. He was going to say something, but Ruby got up to fetch her accordion from a chair in the corner, and began to play quietly. What were they all talking of, this disparate group of people, SA Pete with his stories, Monica with her wild notions, Philadelphia with her longing? Words and sounds drifted through his thoughts.

Gregor had pushed away his plate and was listening to Ruby playing, in that intent way Willoughby had first seen almost a year ago when they busked as the snow had fallen. How much had changed for him since then. When was it he'd started to love Ruby? When she first opened the door to him? When they sat in the café having breakfast together?

'We should go out busking again, Gregor. I missed it so much,' Ruby said, pausing for a moment. 'Listen, what do you think of this?' She ran through a melody, hummed the harmony.

They were bonded in a particular way, as she had often told Willoughby. But he saw it now, clearly—a thread that ran deep, through their parents, through the harsh and terrifying world they'd been born into.

How she played, how he moved. Willoughby recognised what Leda had seen the first time she'd encountered him—that Gregor danced as if hearing another music, beyond Ruby's accordion. Ruby gazed out at them all, and catching Willoughby's eye, smiled her radiant smile, as if she played for him alone.

Sitting on a chair by the gas fire in their room Monica flicked through a magazine. There were bright pictures of other people's homes, kitchens with children and dogs, parcels under the tree. She dreamed of the house she would one day have, when she lived alone, free of the burden of her sister. She thought of how she would furnish it, the shelves of china dancers, the deep sheepskin rugs, a crocheted bed cover in cream and pink. Perhaps she would invite them for tea, Gregor, the child—all of them.

Birdy, behind her screen, sat up in bed, holding a pencil in her hand, Words to describe the night. Nothing—the glow of the gas fire, the wheezing breath of her sister, the light of a passing car—something in her heart—kindness, my love, come my love, come my love…she smiled and gazed out into darkness.

Philadelphia was too good for him. SA Pete knew that. But it didn't matter. What mattered was that there was something to work for now. In the middle of the night, after the dinner, he made a start on tidying his room. He longed to go to her. He would knock on the door, lightly. He would say to her, I'd do anything for you. Just see me, please see my love for you and be kind to me. I ask nothing more. But across the landing, in her own room, Philadelphia lay on her back, sound asleep, her clothes scattered on the floor.

Gregor, in his room at the top of the house, stood looking out at the night.

The evening had been a dream—his lonely misfits transformed for a few hours, sated and warmly drunk. Moonlight had fallen asleep in the chair in the kitchen, and, as he had carried her up to her cell-like room, she'd put her arms round his neck. He'd laid her in bed and covered her up. What would it be like to have a daughter? *Ah, my beautiful sister, her riven face, the baby in her arms—the dead nameless baby.* But that was over. Had been over long ago.

I am German. My name is Gregor von Loeben. I am the son of a Nazi. I believe… Was it over?

It couldn't ever be over, of course. It was as much part of him as the heart that beat under his ribs. But I'll live with it, he thought. I can live with it. As so many others have, and still do.

He imagined a field in winter, long shadows of fir trees over sparkling snow, an explosion of colour, like light falling through glass, so brilliant there were no words to describe, one colour rising through another, inexpressibly joyful.

The boy stood on the deck of his houseboat. It was evening, cold and blue. He was watching the woman who often walked by the river. She stood alone on the bridge. Winter was coming. He shivered. He couldn't stop watching. There was something strange about her. Why was she waiting alone in the bitter wind?

Over her shoulder the woman carried a rucksack. He saw her slip it off, open it, and take something out, a bundle big enough to be a baby wrapped in a blanket. She held the bundle, close to her, on the parapet of the bridge. The river, below her, flowed fast into the sea. The tide was high. Anyone falling in would be swept away.

There was nothing beneath her on the water. She held out her arms and let the bundle fall. A splash—then ripples, wider and wider, as it plunged down into the depths.

What was it, he wondered. If only I knew what she's doing, and where she's going now.

The woman looked up into the night sky, and the boy looked too. No birds flying—only the first star shining above them, and, as they searched, more and more stars, the infinite sky unfolding its darkness.

Tricia Durdey trained as a dancer and choreographer in London and Amsterdam in the late 1970s, and worked for many years as choreographer and dancer. Ten years ago she made the decision to concentrate on writing, and has since had short fiction published by Cinnamon Press, Chester University Press, *Myslexia*, and *Matter* (Sheffield Hallam University), as well as her debut novel, *The Green Table*. She lives in Derbyshire, where she teaches Pilates and ballet.

Also by Tricia Durdey:
The Green Table

When Hedda Brandt and other members of Kurt Jooss's dance company flee Germany for Holland in 1933, Hedda imagines she is going to a place free from the prejudice and threats that have overtaken her country. There she encounters Katje, a girl enthralled by Hedda's performance in 'The Green Table, and who wants to learn to dance.

But Nazi Occupation changes all their lives. Katje watches her brother being drawn into Nazi sympathies, fuelled by his admiration for his German piano teacher, Erik Weiss. And Hedda, faced with regulations that demand that dance should conform to rigid ideology, is drawn towards resistance.

With her life more and more at risk, matters are complicated by the prospect of love with a much younger man, Kai Hoffman, whose family have befriended Hedda. Against a background of oppression, disappearances and terror, Hedda and Katje assert the power of dance, resistance and life in this gripping debut novel that takes real events and characters as its starting point.

Poignant, sometimes harrowing, and exquisitely written, this is an extraordinary story that introduces us to the generation before Ruby and Gregor in *The Dancer at World's End*.

Lightning Source UK Ltd.
Milton Keynes UK
UKHW012017230421
382518UK00003B/170